Copyright © 1981 by John Buxton Hilton
For information, write: St. Martin's Press,
175 Fifth Avenue, New York, N.Y. 10010
Manufactured in the United States of America

Library of Congress Cataloging in Publication Data

Hilton, John Buxton.
The green frontier.

I. Title.
PR6058.I5G7   1982   823′.914   81-14620
      ISBN 0-312-35006-6   AACR2

First published in Great Britain by William Collins Sons & Co. Ltd.

The Green Frontier

JOHN BUXTON HILTON

The Green Frontier

St. Martin's Press
New York

The Green Frontier

CHAPTER 1

The Brigadier had trapped one of the remaining pockets in enfilading fire and the prisoners awaited transport back to the Corps Cage. They would travel by wheelbarrow, his disheartened captives being fallen leaves, of which his Bramley yielded on average thirty-five barrowloads a year. He disposed of them with a certain revengeful satisfaction; not that they actually disgusted him, any more than he had despised real prisoners of war, civilian attached personnel or the wave of refugees who had frustrated his attempt at a strictly localized counter-attack on the road to Dunkirk. They were like fallen leaves, all those people; what else could you expect the poor devils to be but undisciplined? Accepting that as irremediable, the Brigadier in his eighties was mellow and tolerant, so tolerant that he was in fact one of the most liked men in his village. He was liked for his ramrod spine, his pale blue eyes with their hint of aristocracy—and for his unpatronizing willingness to talk to anyone and everyone—whether disciplined or not.

John Devereux, MC (Third Ypres), DSO and bar (Tobruk under Wavell and Sword Beach under Monty), was a sidesman in his parish church but had declined to serve as vicar's warden because, he claimed, that ought to be a native appointment. He could be voluble at the Parish Meeting but would never agree to stand for the County Council because, he said, he could not afford wheels. He was also said to have declined the Lord Chancellor's invitation to sit on the local bench on the grounds that the occasional option of passing a custodial sentence would weigh too heavily on him. It was proverbial in the village that John Devereux would not be able to sleep at the end of any day in which he believed he might have offended man, woman or child.

There was one menacing feature in Devereux's public image, an inclination which made otherwise courteous men deaf, inattentive and pressed to attend to business elsewhere. He could not resist the temptation to bet on any pending alternative and, his raised eyebrows alleging bad sportsmanship, had the talent to recruit a wide circle of takers (he rarely won himself.) He had even been known to make an extempore book on the rival speeds of raindrops running down the window of the Red Lion. It was only his insistence on himself backing a hopeless outsider, heavily handicapped into the bargain, that had got the exercise off the ground.

He was about to return to his offensive when Hedges came down the garden path bearing the look of one torn away from a television racing commentary at a moment of acute uncertainty. Some fifteen years his master's junior, Hedges was a little man, as sapless and brittle as a fallen twig in the beak of a nesting rook. His life had been devoted to the arts of driver-batman, in which office he had officially attained the rank of acting unpaid lance-corporal. But as he had progressed with Devereux from company to battalion to brigade, he had acquired three stripes, all acting and unpaid, and had carried this hallucinatory but useful rank over with him into civilian life. Though not in the academic sense a numerate man, he was in charge of the Brigadier's ante-post commissions and could compute the return on accumulators and cross-doubles with immediate accuracy: a vital gift, for the Brigadier indulged his optimism in the most complex of systems, for which Hedges was never afraid to voice his contempt.

'Yes, Sergeant?'

'Simple Simon half a head behind Signal Light at the third furlong, sir, and there's a young lady to see you. I tried to get her to make a proper appointment, but she makes out it won't wait.'

Devereux rinsed his hands in the kitchen sink and went into the small front room of his bungalow, where sat a young woman who was everything that he regularly and irritably deplored in the contemporary female. Aged in her early thirties, she was wearing dungarees of an emetic Alpine green, with orange socks in wooden-soled sandals. Over the ensemble there hung unbuttoned a shaggy half-thigh-length coat that seemed to be an attempt to recreate in nylon the previous winter's defences of a moulting yak. She also had on spectacles with lenses as large as tea-plates, which it was impossible to imagine could have any effective focal length. Hedges, having effected a grudging introduction, went out of the room backwards: not out of any urge to treat his employer as royalty, but in order to catch his eye with a leer that said that he knew that the Brigadier would be fawning over her in no time.

'Liz Brakeshaft, Home Counties TV, Brigadier. Research assistant on *Crucible*. I don't know whether you watch the programme?'

'As a matter of fact—'

As a matter of fact, *Crucible* was one of the Brigadier's most vehement current hates. Nationally syndicated over the whole independent network, it was everything in late-twentieth-century society that Devereux found most decadent, irresponsible and destructive of human dignity. It pried shamelessly into human confidences, it sneered at the ethics of gentlemen, it derided national leaders and was biased without pretence on the side of the hobbledehoys. Nevertheless, the Brigadier never missed a screening: he enjoyed nothing quite so much as indignation. And there was, he had to admit, a certain cleverness about the programme that did rather tickle him. But therein, he used to say to his friends, lay the danger of it; *they*, of course, were safe enough, *they* could see through it. It was the general run of the public who were in danger.

'Max—our producer—Max Posnan—perhaps you have heard of him? Max is hoping that you'll give us a hand with one of our forthcoming editions. As an expert witness, of course—'

Hedges did not attempt to hide his scorn for the length of time which the Brigadier devoted to Miss Brakeshaft. He did try to hide—unskilfully—his impatience to get on with his summary of the afternoon's results, while the Brigadier was clearly prepared to go on talking about his new interest till supper-time.

'She's to do with *Crucible*,' the Brigadier said. 'They're asking my help on a few little points.'

'I should have thought that at your age you'd have had sense enough to leave that alone.'

'Oh, I don't know, Sergeant. It's about our little show in Holland in 'forty-four.'

'We did next to bugger all in Holland.'

'There were odd moments, I must say, when she seemed a little evasive about the actual theme of the programme. But then, she must be very junior in the organization. Frightened of stealing Posnan's thunder, I suppose.'

'I wouldn't have touched it with a ten-foot dip-stick—sir.'

The severity of that *sir* was the hall-mark of the heartfelt.

'I gather it's to do with the clearing-up operation between the Maas and the Rhine.'

'And there's at least one little story connected with that that I wouldn't want mentioned if my name was Devereux.'

'You're forgetting yourself, Sergeant Hedges. And you

are being narrow-minded and sour. I expect they want someone to keep them on the right lines on the military stuff: sort of technical adviser. Very sensible way of setting about things. *Noblesse oblige*.'

'God help us!' Hedges said.

This was a side of their relationship that the village never glimpsed. It was not that there was anything queer between them: neither of them would have stood for that suggestion for a moment. But each would have said that his attitude to the other was wholly uncomplex.

CHAPTER 2

It was not unusual for a well-heeled foreigner to be caught shop-lifting in the West End of London. The fact that the culprit was a Lutheran pastor from a small town on the Westphalian plain did not impress anyone, either. It was scarcely newsworthy, at least as far as the United Kingdom was concerned. Men could go about biting dogs in late-twentieth-century England without inspiring banner headlines. But what pilfering tourists do not usually do is to attempt to stipulate which detective shall deal with their case: and Pastor Hans Jürgen Pagendarm, held in the manager's office to account for his possession of gold-plated cuff-links, two packets of nylon tights and an inane-looking ceramic owl, demanded specifically that Detective Superintendent Kenworthy be invited over from New Scotland Yard to handle the affair. The store security officer affected not to have heard the request, and sat back to wait for the detective-constable on morning shift. The D-C, when the proposal was submitted to him, entered into no discussion of the issue.

'No can do. Kenworthy retired a couple of years ago.'

Pagendarm repeated his request at various stages of his

processing for court. The station-sergeant had a twenty second laugh about it outside the charge-room. He had met Kenworthy, and was in a position to know how he might have reacted if he had been available and approached.

Clear-cut case: the Pastor made no effort to exonerate himself. Normally, during the season, everything possible was done to bring tourist offenders before the bench within an hour or two of their being picked up. Today the court-sheet was too full for that. And now the polite, unemotional, *korrekt* Protestant cleric further complicated the issue by refusing to sign bail papers, would give no assurance, he made it clear in his obstinately honest way, of his appearance at Marlborough Street the next morning. Could the circumstances of the matter be referred, perhaps, to Herr Kenworthy?

No, they bloody well couldn't. And if this bloody Boche wanted a night in cells, the station inspector said, he could have it and welcome. Do him good to dabble in the wages of sin. Pastor Pagendarm naively asked the constable who brought him his lunch, as a personal favour, for which he insinuated that there might be a reward, if he would privately establish contact for him with ex-Superintendent Kenworthy. The conversation was duly recorded in the Station Incident Book.

The German Consulate was promptly informed of Herr Pagendarm's aberrations and a young official appeared during the course of the afternoon. He was known to the station officers, but not closely: Germans did not rank high in the shop-lifting league. He spent half an hour with Pagendarm, trying to persuade him to accept release until tomorrow's hearing. He came out pouting with resigned frustration. Pagendarm was shattered by his disgrace: he did not want to meet his friends until his case had been disposed of, perhaps not even after that. But would it be possible for a retired officer called Kenworthy to be called to come and see him?

The official pouted again. He had learned to steer an adroit course between his compatriots in trouble and the British authorities, and his sympathies while in the station appeared to be entirely with the latter.

'And at home, you know,' he told the duty inspector, 'he is a very well-known figure. He is the *Radio Pastor*, and has a weekly ten minutes, repeated throughout the Federal Republic. His line is enjoying life within the Christian ethic, and he has a popular way with him. He has thousands of followers who don't otherwise go for the religious side at all. After this, they're bound to have to take him off—even if he could face up to continuing, which I doubt very much from his present mood. And, of course, he comes over here regularly to take part in your *Crucible*.'

'*Crucible*? What's he doing on *Crucible*?'

'He's on the jury.'

The Inspector remembered seeing a German priest as a guest on the *Crucible* team—a panel who asked questions that the producer had put into their mouths. One was an American evangelist who looked like Abraham Lincoln. One was an agnostic don from an Oxford college. One was a nameless English Man-in-the-Street who wore a roll-necked pullover under his sports-jacket and was supposed to flush out all the gobbledegook with a few short, sharp phrases of welcome common sense. And the fourth member came from a pool of more or less exotic visitors: a fleshless *Guru*; a Japanese Zen Buddhist with a frozen smile; a bearded, merry Eastern Orthodox; and— especially in cases with a Central European flavour—this Pagendarm.

'It looks as if friend Pagendarm is going to have to alter his life-style,' the Duty Inspector said, 'unless he's clever enough to make use of this. You know, "I have sunk into the depths myself, brethren—" '

The consular official produced his third and most expressive pout of the day. As a defence mechanism, now that it had this portentous though not quite authoritative witness, the question of referring to Kenworthy was submitted to a higher place. But the query did not occupy much of senior time. The answer was that Kenworthy now no longer had any standing in police affairs and that the German had shown no cogent reason why a tired old officer should be disturbed in his paddock. It was also possible that some among the upper few had no great taste for any re-activation of Kenworthy.

The next morning the German, who pleaded guilty with humbly lowered eyes, was dealt with so speedily that a cynical outsider might have suspected a briefing of the judiciary by the executive. There was not even a moral homily: merely the weary-sounding announcement of a swingeing fine and costs. But then Pagendarm stood rigidly to attention and asked, as if it had been his formal right, yet again for the support of Superintendent Kenworthy. Was the testimony of ex-Superintendent Kenworthy, the Stipendiary asked, directly relevant to the theft of cuff-links and nylon tights? Was Kenworthy, for example, in any position to make a plea for mitigation?

'Nein,' said the Pastor, and then without prompting altered this to, 'No, my Lord.'

'I am not a lord. And I do not see how I am concerned in your request to talk to one of our former senior police officers. Were you proposing to offer Mr Kenworthy as a character witness? Except for this single charge, which you did not contest, your character has not been brought into consideration. It is too late now to change your plea. Would the presence of Mr Kenworthy have enabled you to do that?'

'No, sir. I am guilty.'

'In that case, you are free to take any steps you wish to contact Mr Kenworthy the moment you walk out of this

court. I dare say you will find his number in the Greater
London Telephone Directory. He is a private individual,
and so are you, and we in this country put no embargo on
private social contacts.'

As soon as the fine was announced, a matronly
Prussian in a hat that did not belong to the decade
stepped up to the clerk's table and paid the fine. The
press presumed—and reported—that this was Frau
Pagendarm. She hurried out of the court, as did
Pagendarm himself, but the pair did not come together.
The Pastor pushed past the ambushing minions of the
media, evading even those who had withdrawn to points
of cunning advantage. In the matter of eluding pursuit he
showed a talent for deception which would have done
credit to a much younger man trained in scouting in the
field. Hans Jürgen Pagendarm made his way out of the
precincts of the court, and his mingling with the crowd
outside was almost the last that was reliably reported of
him. In the crowded South West of London Hans Jürgen
Pagendarm vanished from the collective field of vision of
those who had been hard on his heels, many of whom
would have claimed special skill in this kind of chase.

Later the same day, Frau Pagendarm appeared at the
public reception desk of New Scotland Yard, concerned
at her inability to find any trace of her husband. She was
a well-nourished, well-preserved woman in her early
sixties. Her English was fluent though accented, and
doggedly insistent. She received the only answer that it
was possible to give her: that Herr Pagendarm was a free
adult agent in a free country and that ten hours was an
absurdly short gap on which to presume a man missing.
He had had a traumatic experience, undoubtedly a
profound shock for a man of the cloth, and it was highly
probable that he wanted time alone in which to adjust
himself. Details about her husband's clothes and
appearance were noted down as a sop to her persistence.

But she was not impressed by their attitude, clearly disturbed by it, her fingers intertwining nervously. Would they, then, tell her how she could get in touch with former Superintendent Kenworthy, whose name she had been unable to find in any of the directories? What, they inquired in their oblique and diplomatic way, did she think that Mr Kenworthy could do for her that they couldn't? She answered that it was a personal matter, and that Kenworthy was a friend of long standing.

It was the morning after, that is fully twenty-four hours after Pagendarm had appeared in the dock, that a man's body was found alongside a hedge in a pastoral corner of the Chilterns. He had been shot through the right eyeball at short range by a miniature automatic, and his pockets had been emptied of anything that might have helped to identify him. But after his features had been cleaned up by the pathologist, the tell-tale triangle of unshaved whisker over his left cheek was recognized by a mortuary assistant who remembered having seen him on *Crucible*: on a programme about genetic experiments in Ravensbrück.

It was then that Kenworthy was sent for.

CHAPTER 3

Kenworthy was a keen viewer of *Crucible*—though not with that acceptance of its face-values that characterized the majority of its public. It was the producer's nerve that Kenworthy admired—and his technique: the apparent facility with which he could trick a man into giving evidence against himself. Indeed, it was remarkable that some of the leading figures in the programmes had been prevailed upon to appear in them at all. But that was inherent in Max Posnan's genius: he knew the right appeal to vanity. He had a lizard's eye for super-confidence. Above all, he knew when a man's refusal to co-operate might be construed as silent testimony of guilt—when a culprit dared not refuse to challenge the evidence against him. Naturally, there must have been many a project that had aborted in the planning, research or scripting stages; but the general public did not get to hear of those. It was astonishing to many that Posnan had not faced massive libel actions; but this did not surprise Kenworthy. There was always a weight of highly detailed documentation that a man with anything on his conscience would not want to see brought before a public hearing.

Moreover, Posnan was clearly unscrupulous when it came to editing tape. Some of his final offerings must surely have started off in the subject's mind as trial runs, if not as actual buggings. A favourite pattern—the formula was not rigid—was to open with an apparent allegation: the murder of a Catholic in the Falls Road by a former member of the RUC; the adventures of an engaged couple on a municipal housing list; a day in the life of an ex-SAS corporal on his road to recruitment as a mercenary in Zambia; the BOSS man who had achieved the withdrawal of a parliamentary question. It was social indignation with the fuel fed in from high-pressure hoses. It was what the public loved and lived for: the explosion of hypocrites, the stripping naked of fiddlers in high places, the public obligations that had been overridden by feuds, jealousies and bare-faced corruption. In *Crucible* things had a habit of ending up other than they had seemed at first. The plaintive was eventually accused—by innuendo. The humble underdog was the one finally suspected of taking the rake-off. There was an O.Henryish twist, not always in the tail, more usually in the waist of the story: often just before the last commercial break in the fifty-minute feature.

And Posnan rarely underscored the verdict, scarcely more than hinted at it, so that he had the viewer congratulating himself on his own perspicacity. The tables would be turned: the Royal Ulster Constable, his story of an arms cache crumbled, would be seen to be pursuing a vendetta three generations old. The County Councillor with a demon reputation for hunting out abuses was suddenly bracketed between ugly question marks to which Posnan did not give a final answer. Even Kenworthy sometimes doubted his own eyes and ears. Himself a past grand master at the art of turning the world upside down in the interrogation room, he wondered if he could have led some of these wretches on the way that Posnan did. Posnan had missed his vocation as a blackmailer; or perhaps he hadn't.

In the final phase of each edition, the *Crucible* jury summed up their findings, but seldom with a final judgement. Loaded equivocation could be far more devastating. Only in the case of the RUC man had there, by way of variety, been a clear-cut verdict.

Patrick Kerrigan, it does not lie within the powers of this tribunal to offer you the opportunity for penal absolution. All we can do is sentence you to a lifetime at liberty—with your conscience.

It took Kerrigan a fortnight after the showing to pluck up the courage for suicide, whereupon the public reaction to *Crucible* went to extremes—and *Crucible* flourished.

Kenworthy understood all this. But when he was finally called on, and the vain requests of the deceased Pagendarm had been summarized for him, he was perplexed. He remembered seeing the *Radio Pastor* on the jury. Indeed there had been something—a thin, triangular line of facial hairs, high on the cheekbone, which the man did not shave, perhaps because it hid a scar. He could not think when this man's path and his had ever crossed. In his wartime service, thanks to his schoolboy German—which had blossomed in the experience—he had served as a sergeant in military intelligence, and after 1945, in the thick of denazification, he had dealt intimately with the minds (and sentimental remorse) of very many Germans. But he could not recall a Pagendarm. He went through his illicit and barely legible diary-notes from April 1945 to February 1946 and could find no trace of the surname. Indexing his journals had always been defeated by sheer lack of time. Hunting for memories now thirty years old was a laborious business. He could not remember writing or doing half the things that he had put to paper. He was tempted along side-tracks. He found himself ruminating his impressions of Josefina, the adolescent girl-guard from Belsen. He reminded himself of the *Kreisleiter* whose apartment had housed the most pretentious pornographic library he had ever seen: elegant eighteenth-century lithographs of the thirty-two positions. He remembered Kaspar Menschel, the gentle old schoolmaster—and *Ortsgruppeschulungsleiter*—community indoctrinator—who had wept when he had seen the photographs of the death-pits at Auschwitz. But there was no record of a Hans Jürgen Pagendarm.

The case was under the oversight of Clingo, now a Commander, who had been no higher than Chief Inspector when Kenworthy retired. Clingo had always been a plodder, impressionable and ingenuous: had come in from an East Anglian force and never lost the Norfolk lilt in his voice. Clingo had often shown a relish for pomposity—and now he had all the trappings for it. But he also knew, up to a point, that Kenworthy had to be handled with care.

'So if you could somehow pull this one on to the rails for us, Simon—'

'I'll do what I can, Bill—but I can't for the life of me

see where I come into it.'

'His wife—his widow—claims to know you personally. She goes as far as to say that if the arresting officers had taken notice of Pagendarm's requests to see you, he'd be alive and prospering as of now. But she'll only talk to you. I've laid it on for that to happen presently.'

'She rings no bells that I can recall. Maybe under her maiden name—'

Whereupon Clingo gave him an all-boys-together knowing look—and got Kenworthy's frostiest glare in return.

'Sorry, Simon.'

Clingo was an ass. But he had always been straight and clean, which was no doubt why, in the present climate, he was sitting in the desk they'd given him. In that seat, with the word *corruption* no longer even a whisper, they'd rather have someone safe than someone clever.

'Better wheel her in,' Kenworthy said. 'And, obviously, leave her alone with me. I'll tell you in half an hour's time whether we're all wasting our time or not.'

His first impression was that thirty years had neutralized anything individual in her appearance—yet he knew her at once. She seemed to have developed into the prototype of the North German *Hausfrau*, and one who did not drop naturally into this quarter of the century. She looked the matronly end-product of the Gretchens of all time: the standard figure, big-boned, broad-browed, generous-bosomed. Her hair, unattractively greyed, with whiteness not far from taking over, still had streaks that spoke of her prime past as an Aryan blonde. And in spite of corneal veins distended and sore from prolonged weeping, her eyes were still that mixture of intensity, potential charm and busy intelligence. When he saw those eyes, the rest of her slotted into place. And at the sight of him she released fresh tears—together with a flush of soul-felt recognition.

'Ach, Mr Kenworthy—'

He had risen to greet her, and she came towards him as some women might to bury her head in his shoulder. But she was a shortish woman and Kenworthy was a tall man, so it was against his arm, above the crook of the elbow, that she hid her face, at the same time gripping his other arm as if she never wanted to release him again.

'Ach, Mr Kenworthy—'

If he had not known before who she was, he would have known then.

CHAPTER 4

The Brigadier was kept waiting, he thought dis-courteously, for some twenty minutes in an anteroom where low, spindle-legged, highly lacquered tables were littered with magazines, most of them highly technical about the visual arts. Then he was suddenly pounced upon by a perfumed young lady in a white coat who ushered him to a cosmetician's table in a brightly lit cubicle where she proceeded to comb his hair and pat his cheeks with a pink powder puff. His distaste was instinctive, but his protests too feeble. The operation was complete before he became really articulate.

'Actually, I haven't agreed to take part in anything yet. I'm only here for a preliminary talk.'

The girl looked at a schedule that she had on a clip-board.

'John Devereux? You're down here, right enough. Actually, Max often likes to move into a shot or two straight away, and he hates interruptions just when he's ready to start. I shouldn't worry if I were you. Max knows just what he wants.'

Which was, immediately, to keep the Brigadier waiting

for another twenty minutes, and then to come and shake
hands, while looking over his shoulder and carrying on
simultaneous conversations with lighting engineers, a
caption writer and a continuity girl. He did not seem at
first quite to remember who Devereux was, or for what
purpose he had been called, but he took him away into a
studio corner scattered with the remnants of a previous
feature, apparently a kitchen-sink comedy.

'Ah, yes—we thought you might be prepared to lend a
hand with an idea we're playing with for *Crucible*. Hardly
out of the chrysalid stage yet, but we never know what
there is in a project till we've been round it a few times.'

Posnan was a Jew, with tight curly hair, and wore a
navy blue Guernsey with jeans and dirty white tennis
shoes. He had a healthy tan and could have passed
himself off as ten years younger than his actual age. He
was in his late forties.

'It has to do with refugees on the actual battlefield. We
gather that that's a subject on which you've picked up
some expertise in your time.'

Someone behind the Brigadier was clipping a micro-
phone to his lapel.

'I say!'

'Not to worry. The engineers like to try out a few angles
and distances. It saves time later on if they know your
voice-level and overtones.'

'I haven't agreed yet—'

'Of course you haven't. This is only prelims. I don't
even know yet whether we can use you. We have to be so
damned careful, you know, to check facts. And you of
your generation, who were actually on the ground—well,
you're beginning to thin out, you know. Refugees—'

'A menace,' the Brigadier said.

'In what way?'

'You couldn't move for them. They were in your way.
You got your men on the line, sighted your covering fire,

finalized your barrage tables. The next thing you knew, your axis of advance was choked by the peasantry. Women in black weeds with everything they'd managed to salvage in an old pram—including the poultry. Old couples with handcarts: kids bawling and squalling. An old biddy with a goose's head sticking out of a sack on her back.'

Spots and battens were suddenly switched on at all angles, flooding him with intolerable brilliance and heat. He blinked.

'Not to worry. Testing the balance for a sequence we're shooting this afternoon. Everything happens at once in this place. A right rabble, were they?'

'Of course they were a rabble. What else could they be? Didn't know where they were going, couldn't have told you where they'd got to. Nobody in command, you see.'

Somebody tracked up on his flank with a camera.

'Take no notice of them. So you were frustrated right, left and centre?'

'Naturally frustrated. The Hun was driving them into our rear, you see, preventing any counter-action. I wanted to mount something, had a plan, but it meant going straight through the civilian column.'

'Which you fought shy of?'

'Orders from above, old man. Had to call it off. I'd have sacrificed fifty of them to have saved half a brigade—two and a half thousand of ours. That's what war means.'

'And all this happened in Holland, in autumn 'forty-four?'

The Brigadier snorted.

'Dunkirk, four years earlier.'

'But you were in Holland later on, weren't you? Lieutenant-colonel commanding a battalion?'

'That's correct. After the failure of *Market Garden*, when Monty's long plunge had been scrubbed and

Eisenhower's broad front policy won the day. We had the job of mopping up between the two rivers, Rhine and Meuse: Maas they called it, up there.'

'And you were up against the refugee problem again?'

'Not on the grand scale. There were a few line-crossers.'

'But what about those in the villages, caught between the two armies?'

Brigadier Devereux was beginning to feel that he was not asserting himself.

'There was a bit of bother. But look, Mr Posnan, it wouldn't be right of me to be quoted on a military operation without clearing it first with the War House.'

'I'm sure you have nothing to worry about. We're accustomed to handling high explosive on this programme. You can be sure that every line we put out is vetted and double-vetted by the company's solicitors. And if any official clearances are needed, you can rely on them to get them for us.'

The Brigadier digested this and found it reasonable.

'Now,' Posnan said. 'My information is that early in November 'forty-four you and another battalion of your brigade were ordered to clear up a nest of self-propelled guns.'

'That's right. Suicide squads, if you like. Sort of armoured artillery, each gun a mile or so away from the next. All set to lob a shell every half hour, as long as their ammo lasted. Even had the sauce to plonk a couple into Corps HQ. So GS Ops got fed up with it. We were sent to mop up.'

'And I believe you ran into the inhabitants of a starving village, trying to come through your lines with a white flag and get cared for?'

'That was the story. Didn't actually see them myself. Dutch parson came to see me the previous evening. Daren't make him any promises. Certainly daren't let him

know the attack plan. Told him to hold his horses. He
didn't.'

'So you drove down through them? Put a barrage down
into the middle of them with your supporting twenty-five
pounders?'

'That's putting it ruthlessly. It was a question of
arithmetic, don't you see? X lives lost against y lives
saved—where y is ten times x, and happened also to be
my battalion.'

'Could you not have held your attack to let the villagers
through? How much time would that have cost you? An
hour?'

'An hour for the Hun to bring up a line regiment. We
were already off our start-line, so the fact of our attack
was no longer a secret.'

'And these Dutchmen were quite defenceless?'

The Brigadier began to lose patience.

'Young man, you may think you know something of
military strategy, but I cannot think that your
experience—'

Posnan did not rise to the rebuke. From his point of
view things were going well. An interviewee who lost his
cool could be a gift to the script.

'As a mere civilian,' he said, 'I have a sour distaste for
the whole manœuvre. But I do know certain facts that
you don't, and they throw a new significance on the whole
operation.'

'What facts can you possibly know? I will not appear on
your damned irresponsible programme.'

'Calm down, old friend. If you'll listen to what I'm
going to tell you, you'll realize that you were the victim of
a mean trick.'

'How can you talk like that? How can you know anything about it?'

'Two Dutchmen have come forward.'

'After all these years?'

The Brigadier was now sitting askew on the edge of his chair, as if he had decided to get up and go. He remembered his military bearing and squared himself.

'Let me finish the story, Brigadier. Then you can put me right on any military details on which we might have gone wrong. Then I'll take you round to the office and we can draw up a contract. I think you'll have a pleasant surprise when you see what sort of fee we have in mind. This party of refugees, you see, who might have thwarted your advance: they were not all they seemed. Some of them were genuine, including the two who have talked to us. But among the group were sabotage agents, being worked through your line by a German got up as a Dutch priest.'

CHAPTER 5

Kenworthy's mind went back to Christmas Eve, 1945, Berlin-Charlottenburg. It was a grey pathos, virtually total destruction over nine miles square of the capital. And Christmas held a desperate symbolism for a population that lived on without hope. It had suddenly become a matter of urgent necessity for every family, every remnant of a family, to possess a Christmas tree. The black market price of a young pine rose fantastically, and men were prepared to take their lives in their hands to creep out at night into the plantations in the Russian zone to steal saplings. There had been one outrageous case of adolescents dragging a wooden truck who had been shot up by a Red Army patrol.

Kenworthy had been out in the streets in the late afternoon when an unbelievably surviving church bell had tolled. There had been an attempt to mount a small open-air fair in the streets of Charlottenburg: shabby stalls, lit by naphtha flares, with nothing but the tawdriest offerings: spice-cake made with a token dusting of sugar; flimsy, sawdust-stuffed balls on perishing elastic; meagre edgings of tinsel. There was something about that Christmas market that summarized the war: the war had defeated two tyrant regimes—but a lot of people had lost it.

Kenworthy was in no mood for easy persuasion otherwise. He had had enough of everything. He had had enough of being parted from his wife. He had had enough of the bottom-dredged human histories that filled his sixteen-hour working day. He had had enough of a defeated people; enough of the people he worked with; enough of the people he worked for.

There was his comrade-in-arms Marty Roseman, who through every minute of the war had breathed fire and reprisal against all things German, from Himmler to Beethoven, and had now caught gonorrhoea from an ex-Gestapo *Stenotypistin* whom he had been sent out to bring in for questioning from the Augsburgerstrasse.

There were Corporals Clayton and Travis, whose favourite evening occupation was what they called *Exercise Sale and Retrieval*. One of them would go ahead, along the pavement of the Kufudamm and sell a packet of cigarettes at a ludicrously high price to some loitering black marketeer. Thirty yards behind, the other would overtake the purchaser and confiscate the purchase. Kenworthy had sworn that he was going to shop those two buggers even if their court-martial cost the section a sixth of its working strength.

There were his superiors. The OC was home on Christmas leave and they had a stand-in, a university bright boy who hadn't been through the campaign, who tried to interfere, but didn't know enough about it to make his presence felt. He was due to leave them at the end of next week, but the Old Man, who had quite

illegally driven himself to the Channel port in one of the
section's jeeps, could take up to a month to get back,
having calls to make on the way. When he'd had home
leave last summer, it had taken him six weeks to get back;
and then it had been with a pimple on his penis. Inter-
minably he had asked everyone—except an MO—
whether they thought it was VD or not.

There were the Staff, to whom Kenworthy had easy
access, it being grasped in high places what sort of section
this was and who did all the sodding work. Kenworthy
was hail-fellow-well-met enough with majors and
lieutenant-colonels: they were all perfect gentlemen—God bless them. But he could not understand why
so many of these high-rankers appointed to deal with the
problems of the civilian population were without a word
of the German language—and did not seem to want to
learn. And it was uphill work getting them to accept as
urgent anything that wasn't in the manual.

Take the Berlin scientists and technical top-liners, for
example. Two or three nights a week there were kid-
nappings, even in the British sector, and they were being
entrained to Russia. Men—and their wives—came to
Kenworthy's office daily, pleading that it was their turn
next, and asking for something to be done to save them.
Kenworthy reported minute details and put up the
strongest case he could for surveillance or, preferably, for
spiriting them away to the West. No doubt it was all
being discussed, a few hundred miles away; and they
continued to disappear in penny numbers.

Nor could he succeed in stirring anyone about the
British prisoners of war released or escaped from Stalags
in Poland and Silesia, when Rokossovsky's armies were
sweeping across the northern front. Some of them were
still making their way across Eastern Europe on foot,
perhaps shacking up now and then for a fortnight's rest
with a Polish widow. As they dribbled back into the orbit

of British units, they ended up with Kenworthy for screening. He collated news of others in a similar predicament and knew the approximate whereabouts of several who were picking their painful way from X to Y to Z. His reports became impassioned. Was it not time, he asked, that a commission was formed with our Soviet *Allies* (this was before the lowering of the Iron Curtain) to go in, round the poor devils up, and get them out and home? Doubtless the War Office would act in its own good time. You could not expect the Army Council to leap into action on the word of a sergeant.

Useless. Like the Charlottenburg Christmas Fair. And somewhere among the ruins a woman was screaming in childbirth. Kenworthy was moving away from the gloomily lit stalls in the former Adolf Hitler Platz when the bell tolled. And all at once a myriad candlelights twinkled out from the hard-won Christmas trees among the rubble—in half-exposed cellars, in toppling upstairs rooms that had neither doors nor windows. He began to walk towards his office-billet. Two hours' more paper work and he'd go to bed with a book and a quarter-bottle of his Christmas Scotch.

Then he became aware that a couple were watching him. It was something stronger than a sixth sense: the London policeman's training augmented by the stalking soldier's acquired warning systems. The male was a shabby-looking German who looked as if he might have escaped military service by being consumptive; and with him was a woman who, although the evening was cold and likely to become bitter, appeared to be wearing the flimsiest of costumes—something summery at that.

He knew that one of them had pointed him out to the other; and it did not surprise him to be recognized by strangers in the shattered city. His name had been passed from mouth to mouth, among characters bonded by common crimes, common cunning and common despair.

He turned into the Allee where a few surviving villas had been commandeered for Occupation use. The pair crossed the road behind him and followed, keeping a distance that seemed almost respectful. He stood and waited, and since they could scarcely have turned tail without pursuit and investigation, they had to come on.

'Are you wanting to speak to me?'

'Sergeant Kenworthy?'

It was the woman who asked. She was still on the young side of thirty, and might have been attractive if she had not so obviously been suffering from the cold. She was wearing the most peculiar clothes: a sort of sailor blouse with an outsize sash, looking like a flapper from the decadent years of the old Weimar Republic: a relic of the aimless age. But there was nothing aimless in the intensity of her expression.

'You want to see me?'

'I have heard of you from Frau Anni Riegel. You called on her after you'd arrested her husband.'

'You'd better come with me to the office.'

Which they did; and still the man did not speak, walking as if in the last stage of exhaustion, so that they had to adjust their pace to his. And when they reached Kenworthy's HQ, Kenworthy's first reaction was to get them all tea—sweet, strong British Army tea, that always came as an initial shock to Germans. It would bring some sort of life back into their December-chilled limbs— especially, Kenworthy hoped, the man's. Seen in the pallor of the market flares he had looked sick enough. Now, under room lights, there was a greyness about him as of a man who was a corpse already. There was also a swelling over his right cheek that began as a black eye and extended from the lobe of his ear to the corner of his mouth.

'If I tell you that my husband has escaped from Haus Ehrlich and has run the gauntlet of Russian troops all the way from Eberswalde—'

If that were true, it was not surprising that he looked as he did.

'Let him speak for himself, please,' Kenworthy said. And the man came to some kind of life, made a gesture of clicking his heels and pulled himself to a round-shouldered approximation to the military pose of attention.

'Helmut Schultze.'

One of the commonest surnames in the nation: to confirm it, he brought out a civilian driving licence, authenticated by a passport photograph. Kenworthy pictured the woman carefully hoarding their private papers throughout their chequered war. Schultze, Kenworthy noted, was twenty-nine; he had less agility than some men in their sixties.

'How did you manage to get away from Haus Ehrlich?'

Others had, but they were men as nimble of limb as of wit.

'Ja, das ist eine lange Geschichte—'

It was indeed a long story. Kenworthy was well aware that it was the woman rather than the man who was telling it. But he let that ride, at least for this preliminary session. She was telling it clearly and without hysteria. She knew which were the facts that mattered and what digressions to avoid. And Schultze was too worn and dazed to have given much account of himself. Haus Ehrlich had had that effect on stronger-looking men than Schultze.

He had served with the armed forces, an artillery man first in the east, then in Northern France and the Low Countries. When his formation had evaporated, after the Allied crossing of the Rhine, he had taken to the land and bought himself refuge on a secluded farm in the hinterland of Bremen. But such cash as he had about his person could not last long. There was a limited spice to the life of hiding in barns and granaries every time a British unit was approaching—or said to be approaching. Nor was there any sense in trusting the country folk, who could not help knowing of his presence. Someone, sooner or later, was bound to seek favour by turning him in. Most of all he was desperate for news of his wife, with whom he was as deeply in love as a newly wed, and of whom he had not heard a word since the Russians had started advancing with their field-guns up the tunnels of the Berlin Underground. So he had made his way across the German plain by night, relying partly on his army fieldcraft, more effectively on luck and the haphazard inefficiency of the Red Army units that were dotted about the landscape. He fell in with a small group of ex-servicemen on a similar pilgrimage to his own. By day they lagered up in a terrain that was warm, damp and seemingly endless. They stole eggs and ate raw beans and roots from the fields. As they neared Potsdam, he judged it safer to cut loose from his temporary comrades, and it was as well that he did, for within half an hour he heard shots across a maize-field as they ran into the cross-fire of a patrol that was too trigger-weary to have patience for questions and answers.

Schultze reached Berlin, and through a chain of shifty, suspicious contacts found Anna-Maria, who was living with eight families in a bombed-out cellar in the Mommsenstrasse. The sweet homecoming was embittered by mortal fear. His name had to be added to the hand-written list of residents pinned to the doorpost. If the town patrol did a snap-check, he was certain to be taken away for questioning. And not one of the other inmates was to be trusted. One night was as long as he dared stay here; and that might be one night too many.

The next morning, Anna-Maria made him tag along with one of the labour-gangs, making it look as if he had already been allocated penal servitude, as had every able-bodied man and woman in the congeries of streets—

together with many who were far from able. Anna-Maria was crafty; she said the last place on earth where they would look for a man was the place he'd be trying to avoid. But the work was back-breaking, with no prospect of completing it in a millennium: passing along blocks of stone from hand to hand from the rubble of the bombsites. Schultze was next in the chain to a dentist, who complained endlessly that the labour was ruining his professional hands. Politically, the people's minds were in chaos. The Nazi civil command had worked through a hierarchy of cell-leaders, block-leaders, street-group leaders, and the Russians, desperately needing the framework for a local administration, had simply appointed the existing bigwigs back into their jobs. So what had it all been about?

Anna-Maria, meanwhile, who was shifting rubble in a neighbouring block, had assured him that she would find some sort of solution during the course of the day, some safer ruined cellar in which they could lay their heads together. Throughout their fragmentary married life she had come up with occasional miracles.

But not this time. He was arrested before the end of the working day: by two strapping Mongolians from the Red Army's Women's Field Police, who came specifically for him. He had been denounced by somebody in last night's cellar, who had formed the impression that he had served at some time on the eastern front. Hence to Haus Ehrlich.

Haus Ehrlich was the apotheosis of the interrogator's craft. Kenworthy knew, from having screened a previous escapee. With an unpredictable mixture of brute force and sophisticated luxury—and with time and patience on their hands—the NKVD laid bare their subjects. It was the nice-guy-and-bastard technique exploited nearly to perfection, without reference to expense or urgency.

For days Schultze was kept in semi-darkness, with unpalatable, irregular and inadequate meals. There is nothing more disconcerting to a prisoner in the early stages of his captivity than the growing fear that he might have been forgotten altogether. The NKVD got Schultze well into this state. Like his predecessors on the bedboards, he did his best to record the passing of time by a row of scratches on the wall. But he even had to guess at the division between day and night, and reached a state of mind in which he sometimes could not remember whether he had just made a scratch or not. It was a fortnight, he calculated, before he saw anyone but the silent guards who brought him stale rye bread.

At the end of this time, dazzled by daylight, he was brought up into a soulless office, where a Russian captain in aggressively unglamorous uniform (but wearing all his campaign medals about his daily work) hurled questions at him over a scrubbed trestle table. They were routine and simple questions at first and the interview, which filled nine twelve-hour days (Schultze now had the benefit of the captain's wall calendar) mirrored every form that one man's questioning of another can take: a bludgeoning search for information, a ceaseless and twisted repetition of all that had gone before, every opportunity seized for trickery and bewilderment. There were sarcasm, threats, wheedlings, backhand raps across the mouth, lurid insinuations of what had happened to the last non-cooperator. Sometimes his chief interrogator was relieved by a manifestly less patient man who needed to be convinced again of ground already covered.

Schultze was not a fool: Anna-Maria did her best, in the teeth of the visual evidence, to present him as a once brilliant brain. When Kenworthy saw him at the Charlottenburg *Weihnachtsmarkt*, he was physically and mentally at the end of his reserves. He had survived rather more than five months of Communist confusion techniques. He was ready above all else for a very long sleep in white sheets under loving nursing—instead of which, he

had just spent another two cold nights in the ruins of
Berlin. Yet he appeared to have kept his wits about him
in Haus Ehrlich. He did not know who the Russians
thought he was. He did know that if they were troubling
to keep him alive at all, it must be for something that they
thought they could learn from him: and it had to be
something big to warrant the trouble. The moment they
had learned it — or had decided finally that there was
nothing to learn — it would be all in a day's work to do
quietly away with him. Brain for brain, he had to stay as
sharp as any of them were. Perhaps they thought he had
held some sinister position in the secret field police in
Operation Barbarossa. Surely the only information that
they could value from him was evidence that would
enable them to identify some of their own renegades. He
knew that the besetting weakness of the Soviet forces were
the huge patches of incompetence in their communications systems. He stuck to his story: he had indeed
served on the eastern front, but as an artillery corporal.
He stuck to verifiable history when it came to troop
movements and engagements. His account of himself
would stand up to any check that they were able to carry
out.

He got to know his principal enemies at Haus Ehrlich.
There was Gregor, the captain with the stiff leg who was
his chief case-work officer, and who clearly wanted to
keep him to himself and win all the credit. There was the
Commandant of the station, who had to keep his eye on
working schedules and, presumably, some measure of
accountability. And there was a squat *kommissar*, who
seemed to belong to no one, nor anyone to him, and who
obviously had a sceptical eye on everything that everyone
was doing.

They accused Schultze of leading an extermination
Einsatz at Kiev, of taking part in the execution of hostages
at Smolensk, of undercover activities in Viazma-Briansk.

He stuck firmly to his artillery role. He had fought on the southern front and supplied realistic descriptions of the retreat from Cherkassy to the Dnieper. But the captain did not believe him. He suspected something—something which was making him keep Schultze alive much longer than would otherwise have been the case. At last, Haus Ehrlich accepted stalemate. They changed their approach.

Schultze was taken out of his cell one morning and left alone in an upstairs flat—a wing of the requisitioned country property that he had not known about before. The windows looked out northwards over the rolling pine-forests towards Pomerania. There was an absence of visible security of any kind: no guards, no bars. But he did not allow himself to be deluded on that score. Fresh clothes had been laid out in the bedroom; his fit had been well judged. He waited for a long time for something to happen: nothing did. He went into the bathroom, nervously tried the taps, eventually bathed and dressed himself. No one came upstairs to interfere with him. It was as if Haus Ehrlich had been deserted by its inmates. He sat down in a bedside armchair and awaited events. It did not seem that there were going to be any. But at last he heard footsteps, and it was an orderly who stopped and looked at him through the open bedroom door.

'There's no need for you to hang about up here. Why don't you go downstairs and make yourself at home?'

Schultze was too _fly_ to fall for that one. He had not admitted to the knowledge of more than an odd syllable of soldier's Russian—though, he claimed to Kenworthy, or, rather, Anna-Maria claimed on his behalf, that he had an excellent literary command of the language. He feigned incomprehension; the man evidently had no German and did not consider his message worthy of development. Schultze allowed three-quarters of an hour to pass before deciding to explore the lower floor, which he did gingerly enough at first.

He came down to quarters furnished by some vanished German near-millionaire, and though there was no one about, the rooms showed signs of regular and familiar occupation; magazines, both eastern and western, and on a side-table a chessboard with an end-game deployed, alongside a folded newspaper in which the problem had been set. He approached, tried out a few alternatives, had an acceptable solution in less than a quarter of an hour, restored the pieces to their original positions. Music was playing softly on a radio that someone had left switched on: a Mozart concerto — he recognized the *Jeunehomme*, K.271. He sat down and listened, idly turning the pages of an ancient copy of *Der Schalk*.

Early in the afternoon, the orderly came in and began laying the table for a meal. Half an hour later, arguing voices approached and four Russians came in: Gregor, the Commandant, the *kommissar*, and another whom Schultze had not seen before. Places had been laid for five.

And, indeed, Gregor signalled that he was expected to join them. He did so, with discreetly exaggerated gestures of respect. But there was no attempt at introductions. A tureen of vegetable soup was brought, its staple some species of pumpkin. But he had scarcely put his fingers on the handle of his spoon when there were heavy footsteps behind him. Someone was touching his shoulder and four toughs in uniform were making it clear that he was to accompany them. The officers at the table seemed oblivious of the interruption and went on talking to each other as if nothing were happening.

He was led out into a mews yard where his escort surrounded him, each about three yards from his neighbour. And they began to push him from one to the other, thumping him below the belt, crashing fists into his teeth, kicking his knee-caps, stamping on his insteps.

Once, when he stumbled down on to his knees, he was roughly hauled back to his feet and a hand swung across his jaw to shatter his upper denture. Finally, a punch in the solar plexus was followed by a knock-out uppercut. He came to momentarily as he was being fireman's-lifted up the stairs. But he scarcely knew that that was what was happening to him, only that he was hanging upside down, that he was beyond the tolerable thresholds of pain, and that he wanted to be sick. And when he gained consciousness again, he was lying in the bed in the flat, and there was an interval of merciful seconds before the mesh of pain returned.

And there was something else: a woman's perfume such as had passed out of his experience—a woman's cool fingers smoothing his forehead. She was a blonde. He put her in her twenties, but that may have been skill at the dressing-table. She was German: she could have starred in an UFA film of the 'thirties. He was in no state to be sexually excited by her; for her mother-love, whether mocked-up or not, he was unfathomably grateful. He wanted to turn over into his pillow again and sleep; but more than that he wanted to keep her with him.

'Can I get you something? Chicken broth with an egg in it?'

He shook his head. He was in pain from head to foot.

'A mouthful of brandy?'

She went away to get it. She would never come back. She was all part of the stage-managed fantasy. They would come back soon for him, to take him out and beat him again. It was all part of the new treatment. But she did come back, bringing both the brandy and the broth, which she insisted on feeding him as if he had been a sick child, supporting his back between the shoulder-blades with one hand, while she eased the spoon against his swollen lips with the other. Then she went to the armchair with a novel while he slept again. The next time he woke, it must have been late evening, for she had undressed and was wearing peach-coloured artificial silk pyjamas and was about to get into bed with him.

There was no sex that night or for several nights. Schultze did not like talking about such things, was hung-up about them, even in front of Kenworthy, though a glance from Anna-Maria showed that whatever had ultimately happened was placidly understood between them. It was also clear that she understood and was unworried by his complexity of inhibitions. The blonde in the peach-coloured pyjamas had also had a way with inhibitions; such a way that on the fourth or fifth night he had to remind himself that she was a hundred per cent the servant of the NKVD.

He knew what this process amounted to: the bewilderment of extremes. He had heard of other cases where it had happened. He would be given the ingredients of high living, cultural stimulus, music, this woman. And at intervals that he could neither measure nor foresee he would be torn away from these things, thrashed, tortured, terrorized; then restored to his comforts. Within days he would be unable to follow a straight line of thought. And Dora—Dörli, she insisted on his calling her—was only an item in the mad, fabricated illusion. He must not lose sight of her position in the scheme of things. She, like him, could lose her life for a split second's error. Like him, she was probably going to lose it, whatever happened. But not if she could help it. He knew that anything he let fall to her would duly be reported to her masters. Yet this did not seem to be her role at all. She never made any effort, direct or discernibly oblique, to pump him. Her sympathy seemed natural.

He understood the new pattern and its purpose. He was given food, sometimes at table with the Russians, whose amiable conversation among themselves he must show no sign of comprehending. Now and then a meal was served to him and Dörli in the flat, sometimes without interruption; and sometimes he was allowed to reach the dessert before the heavy-duty squad came for him. Once, they forced smouldering splinters under his fingernails, but for the most part the infliction of pain required little apparatus: fifty or sixty strokes across the flesh of his calves with a steel-cored riding-crop. Once, he was taken from Dörli's breast in the small hours—and returned to it after having been beaten with a rattan cane sheathed in rubber tubing.

Only once or twice did he try to prise facts out of Dörli. She headed him off curtly.

'Listen: I know nothing. And I'll go out of my way to go on knowing nothing. It's the only safe way—and even that's dangerous.'

He sighed, almost a convulsion.

'All I know is that men in your position have only one way to help themselves.'

'I can't tell them what they want to know, because I know nothing.'

Dörli often left him for three or four hours in the daytime. It was always an inordinate relief to him to have her back and he tried to remain objectively aware that this was all part of the general intention. Sooner or later, he knew, they would withhold her from him at night; and eventually, for three consecutive nights, this happened. He was disconsolate, had panic thoughts of never seeing her again; but retained enough balance to recognize the symptoms that they were wishing on him. And on the fourth day of solitude there was yet another change in the pattern: he knew that this had to happen, too. A soldier whose face he did not know conducted him along basement corridors to Captain Gregor's office.

'We haven't had a talk for ages. It must have occurred to you, surely, that we are running out of time.'

Schultze made ambivalent noises. He knew that only

too well. Outside in the yard the toughs were probably already waiting with loaded rifles.

'You have nothing to tell me?'

'I have told you everything I have to tell you—many times.'

Captain Gregor shrugged.

'I'd give it a little more thought, if I were you. If you want an interview with me, any time between now and dawn tomorrow, you can ask to be brought to me.'

Schultze nodded. There was no hope left. And Dörli, who came back to him that night, was subdued, not a humour she had ever shown before. She even flinched from physical contact with him. He was flattered into thinking that perhaps he had meant more to her than a mere assignment.

'They're going to kill you tomorrow.'

'That's pretty obvious.'

'It isn't my business—but is it worth while holding out?'

'Have they asked you to have this last try?'

'No. This is on my own account. I've missed you, these last few days—and I thought I was past that ever happening to me again. What is it with you? A matter of politics? *Brown* politics? You don't by any chance still think there's any point in being a Nazi, do you?'

'It's not politics. They'll kill me, whatever. But every day they don't is another day alive. I'm not under the illusion that they'll let me go on living this kind of life indefinitely.'

'You seem to have resigned yourself to it.'

'What else is there to do?'

'You give up too easily.'

'Me? Give up easily?'

He pulled up his pyjama jacket, reminding her of his lacerated back.

'Had you never thought of trying to make a run for it? Their guard strength is ridiculously understaffed. At the worst, they can only kill you for trying.'

'There's nothing more certain than that.'

'It's been done before. A man in May got away with it.'

So she had played the same role with others? The realization hurt and depressed him despite his intelligence.

'Where would I go? We're surrounded by a huge occupation army.'

'You came from Berlin, didn't you? Haven't you friends there?'

'Berlin? Friends? Friends I could only put into the worst form of jeopardy. Even if I could get to Berlin, I'd be picked up within a night or two—as I was before.'

'Not west of the Brandenburg Gate. Didn't you know that the western Allies are now occupying three zones of the city?'

'And how do I get to the Brandenburg Gate?'

'It would cost you money,' she said. 'Nobody does anything for anyone for sentimental reasons any more.'

He could not make up his mind whether or not she had been put up to this.

'How much cash do you think you could lay your hands on? I don't mean here in Haus Ehrlich. I mean if someone could work you into Berlin.'

'I'm not sure.'

Nor was he. He did not know whether he would be able to find Anna-Maria again, how much of her savings she would have left.

'What's it like in Berlin under the new regime? Have you been there?'

'No—but news leaks through. The English and Americans are soft. And there's a regular underground traffic out into the green fields. If you could work your way out beyond Hanover—the main Autobahn check is at Helmstedt—you could get into Hamburg, the Rhineland, the south. Pass yourself off as an ordinary prisoner of war, escaped from the east. You'd be stuck in a compound for a few months, then formally discharged. It's being done all the time.'

'And how do I get out of here?'

'Not by not trying. That's the least of your problems. They have a guard on the main gate, that's all. On the perimeter they rely on dogs. Dogs can be sedated. That much I'd risk for you.'

It was all too slick, too pat, too collusive. He distrusted her. If she was helping him to get out of here, then it was the overall design for him to be got out of here. But why? Not so that they could have the excuse of shooting him while attempting to escape: they were beyond needing excuses. He thought he could guess: because he still had them puzzled; because they still thought he was big; because they wanted to know where he would go, whom he would contact. Was it worth gambling on? The betting on the firing-squad at dawn was a certainty.

'It would be a hell of a risk you'd be taking,' he said.

'Oh, I shall go too. Do you think I've not had my fill of this? But I shan't go with you. I've got a route of my own — but it's one that two don't travel.'

He was sure then that this was a put-up job: too much detail had been thought of.

'So I'm out of the perimeter: what next?'

'Heinz Beuel, out in the village. He has a clapped-out old lorry. And a permit to drive into East Berlin with stuff for the markets. Pretty ropey stuff it is too — frost-bitten potatoes. He'll take you for a consideration.'

'I wouldn't have a pfennig until a day or two after I'd got to Berlin.'

'Understood. He'd lock you away. You'd tell him who to contact. You'd be a prisoner, sort of, until he was paid.'

'And you'd get your rake-off in the fullness of time?'

'I'm doing it without a rake-off — for you. Though I'm

trying hard not to be that kind of girl. The times are too hard for it.'

He did not believe her. Chess was the Russians' national game. It tracked over into everything they did. Pawn takes pawn *en passant*.

'I need time to think.'

'We have no time.'

'Ten minutes.'

'Not a second more.'

He did think for ten minutes, playing out the alternatives in the most vital end-game of his life. Then he agreed. At a quarter to midnight she insisted on leaving him. He did not say so, but Kenworthy assumed that he made love to her a final time, projecting into her a tenderness for him that he needed — and that her skills were equipped to confirm.

At a quarter to midnight she left him, and was gone for an hour and a half. At a quarter past one she came back, by which time he was convinced that he would never see her again, that this was just another twist in the hideous fantasy. She came back as irritable as if there had never been a moment of understanding between them. She bade him get ready, and as he had lost all his portable belongings, that did not take him long. Hushing him at frequent intervals, she led him along a circuitous tour of the passages of the first floor, down into the main body of the house, which was lighted by one dim and distant bulb. The whole place appeared deserted; though upstairs, behind anonymous doors, they had heard the sound of snoring.

She took him out through the kitchens into the chill starlit darkness of the garden. He had never been out here before, saw that it was overgrown and neglected, tall dead weeds tangling over fallen ornamental statuary. She held him still while she listened in the direction of the main gate, and then led him diagonally over what had once been a lawn. He stumbled once noisily into the dereliction of a flower-bed and she ordered him abruptly to stand still. Someone took a pace or two forward from what was evidently a sentry-box by the main barrier and the beam of a torch played elliptically up and down its immediate surrounds. Dörli put her hand on his wrist, holding him motionless until the sentry had withdrawn, writing off the alarum as the product of his imagination. Then she tugged him forward into the darkness.

'At least, we don't have to worry about the dogs. They've had their nightcap.'

So they plodded through the winter-dead grasses, up to a reinforced fence, where Dörli made a gap for them with a pair of pliers—she seemed equipped for every need. They pressed through wire, which clasped Schultze's sleeve for terrifying seconds. Perhaps the worst moment was stepping over the slumbering body of a muscular Alsatian bitch, who heaved up heavily as if she were coming to life. But it was no more than a great exhalation of her drugged breathing. The creature collapsed into herself again, and they were into what might ironically have been called freedom.

They walked along a straight dirt road to the outskirts of a village—so dark that Schultze could form no idea of the size of the place. He had to wait in the shadows at the edge of the road while she drew attention at a door. He heard whispered voices and she came back for him, leading him into a smallholder's living-room in which the paterfamilias was presumably Heinz Beuel. His harassed wife was putting the finishing touches to a packet of sandwiches. A dangerous pair of visitors was no source of pleasure to her, and she took no pains to pretend that they were. The furnishings of the home were impoverished, had been their hard-earned pride sometime in the nineteen-twenties. Dörli went off as if into another room, and that was the last that Schultze ever saw of her. There was no leave-taking, no offering or simulation of sentiment. Nor was there any statement of movement plans. Schultze was made over entirely to the discretion of Beuel, an unsmiling, uncommunicative man who plainly had no intention of talking about the night ahead. Schultze categorized him as of weak intelligence, minimal culture, but of stubborn determination—and with, should it need to be brought into play, a formidable physique.

The lorry was in the last stages of poor shape and could not be far from its last journey—which might well be tonight's. They had a load of winter cabbages, insecure under a tattered tarpaulin. The cab was draughty, its door fastenings missing and replaced by string. They drove for a few kilometres along rural tracks and then came out on a major road whose surface had been pock-marked by tank tracks. They made diversions to circum-navigate shell-holes. There was hardly any other traffic at all: now and then, for long minutes at a time, a pair of headlights stabbing into them down the long, tapering highway between the straight pines.

Then they were being waved down by swinging torches and Schultze took it to be a road-block. But Beuel swore under his breath, and no one asked him for papers. And there was no communication from the Red Army soldiers other than grunts that were in no language at all, but that left no margin for ambiguity. They were made to turn into a forest ride, over a peaty floor dangerously soft under their wheels, a Russian clinging on to either door. They came into a clearing, where they were made to off-load their cargo; and were then allowed to drive un-escorted back to the highway.

'Their commanding officer,' Beuel said, 'will sell that lot for wristwatches on the street black market outside the Reichstag. It happens.'

Schultze assumed that without vegetables there would

be no point in driving on into Berlin, and that his own affairs would take second place. But Beuel said something about having to collect empty crates.

'Keep your head below the dashboard as we drive into the city.'

And so Schultze found himself eventually driven into a yard between rubble heaps, among the desolation of the Schiffbauerdamm. And there Beuel took him into a filthy little cubicle no bigger than the average WC, where he was evidently going to be locked in. It was a disgusting hole, apparently used as a cleaning-store by motor mechanics, for it smelled of sump oil, and the floor was slippery with grease. Schultze optimistically provided details of several channels through which Anna-Maria, or at least someone who knew her, might possibly be traced. But his confidence was wilting.

'How long are you going to leave me here?'

'Until this woman of yours comes over with the amount agreed.'

'But suppose she's no longer in Berlin? Suppose no one knows where she's moved to?'

'In that case it won't be me who unlocks this door.'

Then he was gone and the key turned. There was no daylight except for a high, narrow, barred and grimy window. It was worse than any cell the Russians had ever kept him in. He had no food, and the only water came from a small calibre tap that could hardly be made to drip; and that was smeared with oil. Again, time began to creep very slowly for him, and all but defeated measurement. He made it two nights and three days before he heard footsteps and by then, weak with hunger to the point of experiencing delusions, he could only think that it was some new enemy. But it was Beuel who turned the key and behind him was Anna-Maria, as angry as he had seen her on only one or two occasions in their life together. It was a cold anger, that rough-rode opposition.

She had, she told him later, refused to pay the ransom demanded by Beuel. She threatened to denounce him for extortion — and when Anna-Maria's mind was made up, she got her way. She created such a racket that neighbours began to appear and they were all — for the next vital five minutes at any rate — volubly on her side, even though they did not know what it was about. Beuel folded up: and brought her to her husband.

Her fortunes had changed with the arrival of the western forces. She had had no difficulty in finding herself employment as interpreter-secretary with an English garrison unit, and the officer for whom she worked had had no inhibitions about pulling strings to get her a flat — of sorts — in a side-street off the Kurfürstendamm. It was here that she took Schultze, under cover of evening darkness and spent two days rehabilitating him to the best of her ability on rations wheedled from an army cookhouse.

He had to lie low. In this hungry, deprived, frightened and disintegrated community no friend could be relied on. Anna-Maria broke it to him that that position could not be allowed to go on much longer. Reduced as he was by the last six months to a state amounting to infant unreason, he pleaded with her to let them continue the present state of affairs for ever.

'What do you think they will do with you if they get you again? I can't bear to hear a foot on that stair.'

At midday on Christmas Eve, her office being shut down for the beginning of the holiday, she announced that her mind was made up — made up with the same sort of impregnability with which it had been made up against Beuel.

'We are going to see Sergeant Kenworthy.'

'Who's Sergeant Kenworthy? What can a sergeant do?'

'Sergeant Kenworthy is one of the few men who has an inkling what's going on in this city. Only an inkling, mind — perhaps it's as well for some people that he doesn't know more than he does. But I've met two women whose men Kenworthy has arrested — and they speak of fair treatment. Which of us thought we'd ever use that phrase again?'

'Suppose he arrests me?'

'He will arrest you. We've got to make him arrest you. It's your only way from Berlin to the West. You can fall back on the artillery story that you stuck to with the Russians. But get transported west before they come for you again.'

'And what will you do?'

'I shall know where they are taking you. They are not inhuman, these English. Wherever you go, I shall find a way of following. They'll hold you in some camp for the time being, and I shall be near you. *Über die grüne Grenze* — across that green frontier. People are beginning to live lives again, over there. There are ways and means. It will cost us every penny of our capital — but there's no other way.'

'I couldn't bear to be parted from you for another twelve hours.'

'You'll be parted from me for eternity if you talk and act like a child.'

'We might not see each other for another six months or a year.'

'In Berlin you could be dead within the next five minutes.'

It was not real to him; nothing was real to him. She had not allowed him out of the flat since she had brought him to it.

'We are safe here,' he said.

'Safe? I didn't tell you, did I, that the night before last — since you came home — Drechsler, an engineer, disappeared from the next landing: on his way to the East?'

'You told me there were no Russians left in Charlottenburg.'

'There don't have to be. They come and go as they want. But west of Helmstedt, they have no access.'

'I'm sure there's some better way.'

Then her cold anger took charge of her again.

'Walk down those stairs, then. Cross the Kufudamm. And don't blame me if you never reach the other side.'

So they walked arm in arm up to the Christmas Fair, a new spirit binding them once the course of action was agreed. They were a couple who had had more than most humans could stand of parting, fear and mortal danger. They mattered deeply to each other. They saw their pitiful condition reflected in the shabby Christmas stalls.

'I think that's the man,' Anna-Maria said. 'He fits the description, and I know that's the cap-badge. And he's crossing over to his headquarters. He might not like us to speak to him on the street. Let's follow him.'

In the office that Bill Clingo had lent him, Kenworthy managed at last to conclude his conversation with the middle-aged woman who had twice buried her face in the crook of his elbow.

'You are a genius, Frau Pagendarm. I suspected that when you were Frau Schultze. And is it because he used to be called Schultze that Pagendarm was shot in a field in our innocent Hertfordshire?'

'I can only suppose so, Mr Kenworthy. Oh, if you only knew—'

'I have always thought I did know, Frau Pagendarm. I thought I knew everything, those grey December days in Berlin-Charlottenburg. You have a lot to tell me.'

CHAPTER 6

Max Posnan's location team came out to the Brigadier's village and wanted shots of him taking round the offertory plate in his parish church, sweeping up leaves at the end of his garden, working on his embroidery frame. The Brigadier had had through the post that morning two copies of his contract and its terms, as Max Posnan had hinted, did much to soften his twinges of conscience over the role into which he was trapped.

'But you can't take me being a sidesman until there's another service.'

'My dear chap, we'll have a service, then. Let's borrow a couple of people to be the congregation. A woman's hat and a pair of shoulders in the pew in front are all we shall need.'

And that turned out to be easy, though Devereux could not imagine what the finished product would look like. The business of the leaves, on the other hand had to be re-run again and again before Posnan was satisfied, the garden video-taped from all angles and even his ranks of run-to-seed cabbages photographed like a company drawn up in column of route.

And yet, to the Brigadier's disappointment, the producer was hardly interested in the embroidery, the horses and dogs that he worked on his frame in the long winter evenings. It was only on his own insistence that he had got them into the shooting script at all and he knew intuitively—though he could not have quoted the technical terms—that they were all going to disappear on the cutting-room floor.

Hedges, on the other hand, countered all attempts to involve him with a sprightly, desiccated Cockney 'No comment,' under the mistaken impression that the magic phrase protected him from inclusion. He declined to have himself photographed boning his master's boots. He withheld judgement of his master's embroidery. When asked whether it was true that he had served with his master in Holland, he said, 'Yes, and so did a couple of million others.'

When the team had departed, he spoke to his master with candour.

'And a right bloody twit you've made of yourself today, if you don't mind my saying so.'

'I think you are being unduly harsh, Hedges. Precipitate in your judgement is, I think, the right phrase.'

'After this little lot's been on the air,' Hedges said, 'you'll not have a friend left in the country.'

Devereux generally persuaded himself that abuse from his servant helped to make life worth while. But he did feel that this was not far removed from transcending the bounds.

'Have you ever known me do anything dishonourable, Hedges?'

'Have I ever known you do anything bloody else?'

The Brigadier took deep breaths. He knew it was mess talk that his only tactical plans that had not proved disasters were those that he had first submitted to his batman. An exaggeration; he had, after all, only commanded the brigade for the last four days of hostilities.

'I will bet you,' he said, 'six to four against that nothing comes of this that will be detrimental to my reputation.'

'Done, sir,' Hedges said.

Kenworthy ultimately released himself from Frau Schultze-Pagendarm and attempted to find out by phone the whereabouts of a man he had not met for thirty-four years: a man called Piper, who might conceivably still be

connected with MI5 or that department of the Foreign
Office that is popularly believed to call itself the Secret
Service. He failed to trace him.

CHAPTER 7

'Very interesting,' Sergeant Kenworthy said to the
Schultzes. From what he previously knew about Haus
Ehrlich, he knew there was no reason to reject the tale
that they had just told him. He also realized that it was
easy to believe a story reinforced by the charm of Anna-
Maria Schultze.

She was an intelligent woman, and a forceful one. Her
overwhelming of Heinz Beuel was easily convincing.
Kenworthy also knew that he had allowed the wife to do
most of the talking, a technical weakness in interrogation,
for which he excused himself by the debilitated state of
the husband.

Would the Russians have contrived Schultze's 'escape'
from Haus Ehrlich in this way?

Kenworthy's answer to himself went up through the
progression: possibly—probably—yes, no other explanation. As it happened, it had fallen to him to screen—
debrief has become the vogue word for the process—
another man to whom the same sort of thing had
happened. Presumably this was the man whom Dörli had
mentioned to Schultze, which added credence to his
account. And all-terrible though they were, the NKVD
were capable of monumental blunders. Schultze's
allusions to chess were apt. There were a lot of knight's
moves about—and Grand Masters had been known to
make calculated sacrifices of a knight.

Kenworthy told the couple that he was afraid he would
have to ask them to stay at HQ for a little while yet. He

had a meal served to them from the section's own kitchen: shepherd's pie—that ought to be some sort of lesson to them. While they were eating, he took five minutes' walk round to Staff Headquarters, now manned for the beginning of Christmas by an idling skeleton of clerks.

'Not knocked off yet, then, Sergeant?'

'What else is there to do in this bloody dump but work?'

He went to the *Wanted* index, an idiosyncratic information bank. Sometimes there would be a potted biography that gave a start to an interrogation. Sometimes the brevity of the notes gave the merest hint of a war criminal's past. There were a couple of dozen SCHULTZES, but one which admitted of no doubt whatever. It had in the top left-hand corner a full-face photograph—a print from the negative that had supplied Schultze's driving licence. Such miracles turned up in the index now and then. There followed a scanty legend:

SCHULTZE,   Helmut   SS HStuf   Minsk 43

Not a syllable more: but that note of rank, place and date was enough to seal a man's fate. It meant that there was a hefty dossier on him somewhere: in London, perhaps— more probably in Moscow.

Kenworthy went back to his office. Most of the processing of Schultze would be done far away in the background, at leisure, by the war-lawyers. Kenworthy's role, as arresting NCO, was limited but vital. There was the question of identification, in this case beautifully simple. There was the all-important initial statement in which, under skilled guidance, a man might incriminate himself of more than the war-lawyers already knew. And there was anything that might be drawn from him about the last-known whereabouts of his equally *Wanted* associates.

Kenworthy's first action, out of sight of the Schultzes,

was to steam the portrait off the licence and paste it at the head of a wad of waste typescript, which he then filed in a cover that he prominently labelled. He then went back to the Schultzes and talked to them amiably. He had learned a lot about interrogation since he had been called up from the Met—and since the training that the army had put him through. There were some in the section who gloried in the opportunities to show themselves tough, even genuinely clever. It had been borne in more and more deeply on Kenworthy that it was detachment that counted—the detachment of utter hypocrisy. In fact, hypocrisy was hardly the right word for it. It was a sort of perverted sincerity. He had appeared to make friends— got under their wretched skins—with some of the lousiest bastards in the war crimes archives. Bastards? It was hard to look at Schultze and think of him as anything but a sufferer—one of the stubs of sodden straw that got itself caught in the weir. Yet if the man had been an SS Captain on the lines of communication of the eastern front in 1943, he had something to answer for. His driving licence photograph wasn't on an index card for nothing.

'*Ja*—ordinary people are carried along by the current.'

That was Anna-Maria talking, a woman in command of herself, spotting in Kenworthy his powers of empathy, showing him as their eyes met that she had confidence in his decency. Any moment now he would move in and crush her. He opened the file, let her catch sight of the portrait and typescript—upside down.

'*Ja*,' he said. 'Now let's talk of Schultze of Minsk.'

It rocked them. He saw the terror take over Schultze's eyes. But Anna-Maria summoned up enough aplomb to dissimulate shock.

'*Ja*, how did the Russians not get on to that in Haus Ehrlich? Oh, they are not so clever, that lot.'

'They'll know all about him next time,' Kenworthy said.

'Ach, but you wouldn't pass him over to them.'

'Why not? Where else ought he to go?'

'It would be a terrible waste of a man. When you learn, Mr Kenworthy, how much he *knows*—how useful he can be to you.'

'Useful?'

'Isn't it true—hasn't Churchill known all along—that you were fighting the wrong war? Isn't it the greatest tragedy of this century that your people and mine should have fought to destroy each other? While all the time we have known where the true menace lies?'

It had surprised Kenworthy how open so many Germans had been, even within hours of the cease-fire, in their belief that the ultimate East-West conflict could not be more than a few months delayed. Hadn't Hess been right, in his flight to England in 1941, to plead for a re-alignment in the mutual interest?

'You're sheltering behind a wishful illusion, Frau Schultze.'

'It is over two years since *mein Mann* was recalled from the Russian front. He also served in the west. He has much valuable information for you.'

'About the activities of an SS Hauptsturmführer?'

'Ach—what's in a label?'

Kenworthy opened the typescript again, turned a few pages, pretended to read a paragraph here and there.

'Yes: so he was in the West—with a deal to account for. Helmut Schultze, I am arresting you—'

It was then that Frau Schultze came and clutched at him, buried her face in his elbow for the first time.

'Oh, thank God! The only place where I can know him to be safe. But promise that you will not hand him over to the Russians until you have made the most comprehensive enquiries. Tomorrow he will be less tired. He will be able to talk to you on his own account. I am at your disposal. I will come to this office as often as you like.'

*

Tomorrow was Christmas Day and there were parties—a prolonged section piss-up that it took Boxing Day to recover from. Schultze was put away in the remand wing of Spandau prison. When Kenworthy had him brought back to Charlottenburg after the festivities, he spent the first hour or so acclimatizing him to civilized treatment. It was not the same thing as the mixed-up handling of Haus Ehrlich. Here he could be certain that he was not going to be knocked about, that he would have regular meals and be treated with dignity, even if a criminal. This side of things even had to be exaggerated. He was not an easy man to reassure, but his confidence built up slowly as the day progressed. Kenworthy left him for an hour or so with a packet of cigarettes in a pleasant waiting-room while he got on with the paper-work of other current cases. Anna-Maria had come to the outer office at half past eight this morning. He sent her away until the early evening, telling her that she really could not expect to sit in on every stage of the examination of her husband. She understood, and appeared to appreciate the uncomplicated manner on which he stood on plain truth with her. Already she was treating him as a friend, and he wondered how far she would let him go with her—in the interests, of course, of her husband—if he were to show inclination.

It was an ideal situation for the classical interrogation. Seldom had an investigator been so well placed to play off one against the other. There was no more chance for collusion between them, and any story on which they had previously agreed could be broken down by ceaseless harping on detail. Kenworthy was faintly amused by the way in which she was still trying to feed her husband's story.

Ask him this . . . ask him that . . . ask him the other . . .

Schultze himself was slow to become a fluent witness—as was to be expected. It was clear that in his

prime he had been a shrewd operator himself, and for the
first three long sessions he was obsessed by the fear of self-
incrimination. Kenworthy was patient. He had time. And
as he carefully let fall vital points that he had learned
from Anna-Maria, Helmut Schultze became resigned to
the fact that the greatest self-incrimination in
Kenworthy's eyes was an attempt to hide anything. The
watershed came when Schultze was prevaricating about
his real reason for being in Minsk; and Kenworthy lost his
temper—not merely histrionically.

'Look—if you're not going to play straight with me, I'm
not going to go on bothering. I pick up that phone, I get
on to the Kommandatura, and the NKVD will be here for
you within the hour.'

*'Ja, das ist schwierig. Das lässt sich nicht allzu leicht
dazu gewöhnen.'*

'You'd better get bloody used to it quick, then. I can
dispose of your case in half an hour, if I want to.'

And, once he had pushed himself past the barrier of
the first honest admission, Schultze found it easy—even
comforting—to talk and go on talking. Kenworthy talked
to Anna-Maria, too—for two or three hours daily for a
week. And the fundamental story emerged.

Helmut Schultze had been born in the last years of the
First World War in Koblenz, the son of a corporal of field
engineers who had been killed at Verdun. He was very
much a mother's child. Frau Schultze was without means,
and without either the imagination or the will, to elevate
herself above the most menial ways of maintaining a
home. She kept them barely above poverty level, but
always within the bounds of working-class respectability.
She was also a devout Roman Catholic and the boy came
quickly under the notice of the church, particularly of a
humourless neighbourhood priest, Father Siegmund, who
quickly spotted his intellectual potential, took possession

of it to the point of monopoly, and exercised it ferociously, without offering it any nourishment outside the limits of orthodox theology and ecclesiastical history. There were long walks along the Rheinufer, or they would sun themselves on one of the benches of the Deutsches Eck when the priest was free between offices. The boy's mental strength lay in his vivid, rapid and hundred per cent recall and he had a talent for accurate and finely distinguished classification of all he remembered. His brain, together with a certain quaint priggishness, made him an object of torment among other boys of his age and whenever he could he withdrew from human company to the books that the priest copiously lent him. As a result, he was earmarked for the church almost before he had made any decision of his own on the point, and when the moment came for actually making the choice, he was in a phase of adolescent religious fervour which left him with no real choice to make. Consequently he was submitted in his late teens to the rigours of a theological Seminary and his mother, who was by then a walking cancer case, wept with ecstasy at his ordination.

He emerged into the junior priesthood in one of the inner Cologne parishes in the year that German troops marched into the Rhineland for the first time since the Versailles Treaty. He was a spare figure, proudly upright in his soutane, the object of admiration by young female communicants who ought to have known better—and was almost totally innocent of any understanding of politics, social nuances or the most elementary of commercial tactics. He loved nothing except his God, the symbolism of his church and his spiritual role: until a young parishioner called Anna-Maria Kummerfeld raised her eyes into his life.

She did, literally, raise her eyes. He was turning from the altar with the chalice held high when he looked down and saw her eyes looking only at him: a madonna's face. His ideas of beauty in the female form had been largely conditioned by the often sadly inartistic statuary that he had lived with in holy places. The unknown girl in the fourth pew was almost his first lingering consideration of flesh and blood.

She came back into his mind—sinfully, he knew— many times in the next day or two. He set himself rigorous spiritual pennances, but something held him back from referring his aberrations to his confessor. The second confrontation happened as he was following an acolyte with the Host to an old pauper woman who was dying in a slum in the Hundgasse. Anna-Maria Kummerfeld came by the merest of chance in the opposite direction and again caught his eye, this time so directly that he stumbled over his own toes, and only saved himself from falling by grasping at the surpliced shoulder of the boy. She came forward as if to save him, and actually had her hand on his wrist: a warm and communicative hand— flesh and blood again. But she withdrew it as soon as she saw that he was not actually going to fall. She smiled at him, intensely and personally—and with a vitality that he had never encountered in cell or cloister. He smiled back at her, then turned his face away, blushing hotly. He vanished from her view as he followed the acolyte into a dingy courtyard surrounded by the doors and staircases of hovels.

On the afternoon of their third meeting he was walking along the Rhine bank, reading his breviary, his eyes lifted every few seconds to watch his path. In fact he was hoping, as he always did hope, to meet some child to whom he could talk as Father Siegmund used to talk to him. Instead, it was Anna-Maria who came up to him, apologizing for interrupting his meditations and asking if he had time to discuss a small problem in ethics with her.

It was no teaser: simply a question of telling a white lie

to an invalid. He answered at far greater length than the question demanded, propounding opposing points of view with great solemnity, his pulse beating so embarrassingly fast that it seemed to be affecting his breathing.

They walked together a couple of hundred yards, as far as the next major cross-roads, and when they parted she gave him a little wave, exactly as she might have done if he had been some friend with whom she worked. It was the first time that he really knew, as fact rather than as mere idea, what he had sacrificed. There had been no sacrifice in giving up what he had not experienced. He had lived through his youth without acquiring a taste for anything but the course which had closed round him as if pre-ordained. He had a sense of pharisaical pity for laughter in cafés, for the plots and aspirations of the cinema screen, for the couples who fidgeted in the back seats of young people's meetings. Such urges as he had experienced had even been a kind of joy to him, so far removed were they from realistic temptation, so impersonal and weak that they convinced him of his own spiritual strength and dedication. With Anna-Maria, it was different.

The couple did not tell Kenworthy any detail of their courtship. He did not ask how, when and where they had progressed through the riverside meadows of their Rubicon. It would have been bad tactics to have asked; but his imagination played with likely scenes. As far as Schultze was concerned, relative trivialities—the brush of a fingertip, a tress of hair stirring in a breeze, the new familiarity of a perfume—could have blown up very large.

Certainly the impression came over at this stage that the young priest's relationships were not good with some of the other clerics in the parish. He was disillusioned by the less than saintly laziness of some of the older priests, alarmed to find a streak of cynicism in others. Among

others he was rather a laughing-stock for his often
recondite scholasticism. It should have come as no surprise to him that many priests were far removed from an
academic outlook. And there were undercurrents in the
parish between those who looked on the Nazis as the only
viable saviours of Germany, and those who were far-
seeing enough to fear the ultimate. Each side waited for
Schultze to reveal his own alignment; and the truth of the
matter was that he really had not any. Politics, internal or
international, did not interest him. If he had any opinion
at all about the Nazis, it was one which he kept to himself, and was based on the fact that his mother, who had
known the movement really only during its canvassing
years, had regarded the Brownshirts as a vulgar rabble.

Kenworthy did not doubt that it was Anna-Maria who
set the pace. She was recklessly in love with the young
priest, and the conflict between his vows and mortal
living could obviously have meant nothing in her range of
values; though she did her best to protest, soulfully and
not believing that she could be doubted, that in their
weeks of indecision she had suffered, though in a
different way, every whit as cruelly as Helmut.

However that might be, mortal living won the day.
They fled from Cologne. They were married in the civil
offices. They honeymooned briefly in the Mosel valley on
a couple of hundred marks pooled from their petty
savings. The seclusion of the castle courtyard at Cochem,
the sharp, dry wines of Piesport and Traben-Trarbach,
the idyllic boat-trip to Beilstein were followed by shirt-
sleeved reality. They were agreed that Cologne was
barred to them. He had no job; her prospects were better
with shorthand, typing and the elements of book-
keeping. He brought up old-fashioned ideas about an idle
man living on a working wife, the subject of their first
major quarrel. But in the event, she found that she had
over-estimated her chances. There was a trap: she

became pregnant, suffered extraordinary bouts of sickness in the first weeks and then miscarried. There followed weeks of hunting vacancies in the Ruhr towns. Their reserve savings dwindled and next month's rent, payable in advance, became an empty laugh. Schultze traipsed in vain round libraries, offices and even shops. Their world drained of hope, he descended into gloom, seeing this as the beginning of his eternity of punishment. There could be no release for him on earth—or after.

Anna-Maria was less concerned with eternity, more with the present. It was not tragic guilt that occupied her, but the necessity for an income of sorts next week. She found Helmut a job and pushed him into it: and for the first three days it held promise, while he was being taken round blocks of affluent Düsseldorf flats learning the mixture of flattery and opportunism that sold personalized stationery from door to door. After that he was on his own, and allocated a working-class area in Krefeld, where the only letters that were sent were written on lined note-pads from cheap stores. Schultze had not the charisma to follow up a canvass. He had not the thickness of skin to go on trying after initial signs that he was not wanted. He had not the nerve to develop the ploys that his mentor had tried to teach him: like dropping a hint about the woman on the lower floor who had placed a substantial order. The only woman who asked him in for a coffee did so solely out of pity for his frozen, hungry look: and even she was not interested in what he was trying to sell. His pay, whose astronomical potential had been stressed at his first interview, was derisory without commission. At the end of his first week he was given a warning; at the end of his second he was sacked—and told what he owed the firm for a broached sample that they said was no longer usable.

He came home that evening convinced that the foundations of his life with Anna-Maria were unredeemable.

But he found her nearer her normal self than at any time since her miscarraige—comforting him about a world with which he was blamelessly incompatible. And she showed him an advertisement, copied out from a newspaper in an acquaintance's flat, that could be the answer to every problem that assaulted them. It would mean going to Berlin if he were called for interview, and goodness knew how they were going to find his fare for that. It would mean staying in the cheapest hotel in which a night's rest could be had.

The post was for an archivist for a company that produced technical and professional directories, and whose newest venture was to be a comprehensive guide to the priesthood in all the churches of the country. Meticulous detail was called for, together with a studious temperament and university training in history or a related discipline. Anna-Maria helped him with his letter of application, actually redrafting it for him in workaday language: she laughed at him in her happy manner of old, saying that his prose read like Bismarck's. They went out together to post his letter—an evening walk with a spice of conspiracy behind it, rather like some of the clandestine outings of their courtship. There were one or two pre-1914 household inheritances from his mother that they were able to pawn to pay for the trip to the capital. And in spite of their poverty, Anna-Maria travelled with him to Berlin, the extravagance justified by two considerations: he could not bear to be parted from her, and she was beginning to doubt whether he could find his way across a strange city without surveillance.

He got the job, found himself working under a pleasant, middle-aged office-manager called Stauff in premises near the Berlin Zoo. The work pleased him. The first phase at which he was set was the processing of biographies submitted by the clerics themselves. It satisfied his imagination, reading between the lines of their *curricula vitae* and, thanks to his extraordinary memory, he began to build up a mind-world of personalities, lifestyles and promotional cycles that made him into a kind of human work of reference. Stauff taught him the mechanisms of indexing and he began the nucleus of a closely cross-referenced card system into which was fed information from new sources: theological colleges, individual correspondents, press reports of church functions—and of cases where erring priests had found themselves in unwitting trouble with the law.

They gave him a small advance on his salary, but it was not until the end of the month that he received his first official cheque. And this was accompanied by a machine-processed pay-slip that he brought home to Anna-Maria in some consternation.

'*Herzchen*, I don't know how I'm going to tell you this, but my income is coming from a government source. I came across the reference code in another context the other day—and I appear to be working for the Gestapo.'

To his surprise, Anna-Maria gave the girlish little giggle that he associated with the early, wicked Cologne days.

'Good for you!' she said. 'Now maybe we shall not have to look back.'

'But the Gestapo—'

'Keep your voice down,' she said. 'These party walls aren't much thicker than the paper over them. Listen: The Führer says his Reich is going to last a thousand years, and I won't quarrel with him over five or six hundred or so. Just look what he's done in three years—it's obviously going to last our time, isn't it? So if you've got in at this level while the world is still in the making, there's no telling where you might end up.'

Anna-Maria got herself fresh work shortly after that: in the Small Ads reception office of a Berlin daily. Their finances rose to an adequate plateau that felt like wealth.

They moved out to an apartment in Berlin-Dahlem. Schultze became aware of the sensitivity of the records he was building up. He knew now that there had never been any intention of publishing a directory. The biographies voluntarily submitted began to occupy progressively less importance in his priorities. For three months he was told to hunt out information about those who had submitted nothing on their own account. Sometimes he was called in to committee meetings with laconic men and established a gratifying reputation for producing immediate factual answers to sudden questions. A Protestant pastor on the residential outskirts of Hamburg had come under suspicion for distributing a mildly disturbing pamphlet after morning service: *The Church—of the State or of Christ?* Schultze provided from memory a list of those who had been his college contemporaries, knew what students' clubs he had belonged to, what minority groups he had been associated with in his church. Sometimes he grew moody when he thought of the purposes to which his researches were being put. Stauff, always decent, never less than astute, was quick to notice this.

'What are you worried about? Which is better for our nation: a state in which church and party know they can rely on each other? Or running warfare between the two? Believe me, the work we are doing here is vital if the churches are to survive at all.'

'You must understand, Sergeant Kenworthy,' the woman in the sailor collar said in the Charlottenburg office, 'that a man disgraced from the Catholic Church was an absolute gift to the security services. Especially a man of Helmut's gifts.'

'You must realize, Mr Kenworthy,' Frau Pagendarm said, thirty-five years later, in the first long interview after the murder of her husband, 'that a man of Hans Jürgen's talents was just what the Reich security service was waiting for.'

'You slip fairly easily into calling him Hans Jürgen,' Kenworthy said.

And she smiled sadly in mid-grief.

'I knew him as Hans Jürgen almost three times as long as I knew him as Helmut,' she said.

'Tell me another thing. That costume you were wearing, when you came to see me on Christmas Eve, 1945 —'

She was amused — almost a return to the girlish giggle.

'That was at Hans Jürgen's special request. I had kept some of our personal possessions in a cache in Berlin. We were going to be parted — *you* were going to part us. He wanted to see me dressed as I had been the first time we met. It helped to persuade him to come with me to you. I don't know whether you realize what a sentimental soul he was.'

'It was a cold day for summer clothes.'

'A very cold day.'

CHAPTER 8

One day early in 1937, Stauff took Schultze for a drink on their way home from work and asked him if he had not thought of joining the SS. Schultze found the idea comic at first, but Stauff let it be seen that he was serious.

The SS was always an élite; there had been the frightful Night of the Long Knives when the rival SA was emasculated. But by 1937 the Reich had a substantially more permanent look in the eyes of respectable men than it had had in 1933. The denazifiers of Kenworthy's vintage used 1937 as a rule-of-thumb to judge the degree of fanaticism that might lie behind a man's taking an SS commission.

Whatever might come to light about its wearers' atrocities, the SS uniform, black, set off by silver-white piping, with its half-skull cap-badge, was a paragon of smartness and macho: except on Untersturmführer Helmut Schultze, the first time he put it on. Anna-Maria laughed in a manner that hurt his feelings at first. He was the sort of civilian who could make the newest and most chic of para-military uniforms look as if it had just been slept in. But she showed him how to tilt his cap at an arrogantly rakish angle, how to tighten his belt without making his tunic look like a pyjama jacket. And on his first evening in his new outfit, she insisted on being taken out into one of the most fashionable restaurants in the city. Salutes were flung up at him on the broad pavements: even on pedestrian crossings.

In autumn 1938, now Deputy Director of the Büro am Zoo, Schultze was transferred to a headquarters off the Alexanderplatz and given the direction of a department that seemed to have devolved into half-hearted inefficiency: a survey, again with detailed attention to careers and connections, of the state of the churches in Belgium and the Low Countries. He was appalled by the haphazard work that had been done on the project so far, lost no sleep over contriving two dismissals and a couple of advantageous transfers. By the New Year, his Abteilung was on a sound footing. Now it was Anna-Maria who was disturbed by the prospects.

'When I think of the possibility of war—'

'If it is forced on us by the machinations of Jewish financiers in Paris and London,' he said, 'we would be insane to be found unprepared.'

'And some of your parson friends on your index cards are going to wish you had never been born.'

'The object of military counter-intelligence is to save lives—our soldiers' lives. The price for that needs cool calculation.'

Schultze was learning his brief—and believing it.

In the spring of 1939 he was assigned to produce three lists of local priests for the information of forces advancing from the German frontier to the Channel ports: a white list, a grey list, a black list.

He did not actively enter the field until well into the autumn of 1940 when, as if it were a touristic reward for services rendered, he was assigned nominal duties in Paris, where Anna-Maria was allowed to accompany him. Before the end of the year, he was seconded to special duties in the Campine of north-eastern Belgium, where his smartest coup led to the arrest and execution of a Benedictine monk who had been active along the escape-line of stranded Allied pilots. For this he received a special commendation from Himmler's own second deputy.

Now he was promoted both in the SS and in his department and sent back to Berlin with the challenging assignment of producing a brief for the planners of OKH, the supreme command, on the resistance potential of the Russian Orthodox Church. For this he took a crash course in Russian—and developed an enthusiasm that totally consumed him. When the war on the eastern front started, he was sent out as an adviser in the field.

Hence Schultze of Minsk. The power of the Russian priests in organizing partisan terrorists in the overrun territories took local commanders by surprise—took even the Kremlin by surprise, to the extent that relations between the church and the state underwent a remarkable change for the better. But Schultze's main concern was with neutralizing resistance *in situ*—or, to be more precise, with providing the information on which such neutralization was based. If he made zealous mistakes, they were errors faced up to for the sake of the German forces' security. The *Einsatzkommandos*—the extermination squads operating in Nazi-occupied Slav territories—worked from lists drawn up in Schultze's office. It was only by miraculous inefficiency that Haus Ehrlich had not stumbled on to the connection; or perhaps, even, they had stumbled on to it. There was no analyzing the poker-faced strategy of the NKVD.

'Wheels within wheels within wheels,' Kenworthy had muttered in Charlottenburg. 'Counter-counter-counter.'

'And after Minsk?' he asked Schultze.

'*Ja*—after Stalingrad the front crumbled. Winter on those Russian plains was indescribable. I cannot do justice to the cold. The French use the phrase, it would split stones. I think that was the nadir of my life. It was getting on for two years since I had seen Anna-Maria. The news of the Allied air raids, of which I had some inkling, but which was being suppressed from the ground troops, was deplorable. One saw no end to it. Then suddenly I was recalled to the west—along with many thousands of others, to reinforce the last defences after our Seventh Army was destroyed in the Battle of Normandy. I was attached to a fighting formation now— a divison of Waffen-SS in Gelderland—eastern Holland, after the collapse of your Arnhem bridgehead.'

Where he had come face to face with Brigadier John Devereux—

'*Ja*, Mr Kenworthy,' Frau Pagendarm said. 'Hans Jürgen, when he was Helmut Schultze, undoubtedly did a few things for which he might be held to account. But what was he, other than an ordinary patriot, serving the cause of his country's armies—armies latterly facing the ultimate peril? Did he do anything that you wouldn't have done in your own somewhat similar job? What did you do with spies and saboteurs when you captured them? You are not going to tell me that you did your best not to capture them? Was no one ever hanged in your Tower of London? Was it not only by an accident of birth that your roles were not reversed, yours and Hans Jürgen's?'

'I have always felt remarkably complacent,' Kenworthy said, 'about any accident that attended my birth.'

CHAPTER 9

By the third week of January, 1946, Kenworthy had reached that stage at which a decision had to be reached on the Schultze file. A comprehensive summary had to be made, a recommendation implied and the papers forwarded, together with Schultze himself, for further disposal. It seemed inevitable that he would have to go back to the Russians. Could a case be made out instead for referring him to the French, Dutch or Belgians? It was doubtful whether they'd even have his name on their records. They could not be expected to know all the backroom personalities of the counter-resistance.

There was no more to be gained by further questioning of Schultze, or of Anna-Maria, whose volubility in defence of her husband continued unimpaired. The issue had now devolved into an interesting story, but not a vital one. Kenworthy knew that he was wasting time—but he went on wasting it, as if there still remained something to play for. There were still features about which he was curious, and he went one evening unannounced to Anna-Maria's flat off the Kurfürstendamm. She was, he thought, rather startled to see him, but covered it up with all the appropriate reactions of pleasure. But she was more preoccupied than usual, and in her typically forthright style she was telling him her new troubles almost before he was seated: her flat was, by Berlin standards, a superior bed-sitter, with tiny kitchen and bathroom annexes, and the bed was concealed under a tightly-drawn coverlet with a twee arrangement of asymmetrically scattered cushions.

Not for the first time in her life, she was up a new cul-de-sac of trouble. Like many others at this stage of the occupation, the commanding officer of the unit for whom she was interpreting was employing her unofficially, without having sent her for security screening in the normal way: otherwise, ironically, her name would have been referred to Kenworthy's office for clearance. But as soon as her colonel had heard—by the usual anonymous denunciation—of the arrest of her husband, he had dropped her as if she had been a venomous reptile. Perhaps it was one of the worst spots she had found herself in; but Kenworthy did not doubt that she would survive. She might even have to leave this flat; but she would be installed in another within a month. There was a confident resilience about Anna-Maria.

She had been getting her supper ready, and she pressed Kenworthy to share it with her. It was a crying disgrace to make an inroad into a Berliner's rations at this time, but Kenworthy stretched a point. Potato soup: simple enough but delicious, and he did not decline a second helping. Then they settled at either end of a settee; and he had brought a bottle of John Haig under his greatcoat.

She half closed her eyes and then opened them again in contented acceptance of the remainder of the evening. He wondered whether she would allow him—encourage him— to sleep with her. He didn't want it, didn't intend to allow it to happen. But he wanted to know. He had the idea that she thought that that was what he was here for. But she wasn't certain, and she hesitated to take the initiative.

And she really was an attractive woman, as if both her charm and her physique had been proof against five years of adversity. Kenworthy looked at her, made sure she saw him looking at her, and then looked away as if he were resisting temptation. And indeed, he reflected, it would be easy to let himself go for the first time in the war. He did not think there was much danger, but he felt himself hovering; and Anna-Maria, knowing that he was hovering, waited without noticeable reaction. They had said that any man who slept alone on Liberation Night in Brussels had heen nothing but an exhibitionist; well, Kenworthy didn't claim virtue—he just hadn't wanted it. He had a wife at home for whom he longed as fervently as Schultze had ever longed for Anna-Maria in Minsk.

'*Ja*,' he said. 'Well, I don't think we shall be holding your husband much longer.'

'You know what is going to happen to him?'

'I could not know that. It is not my decision.'

'But they will depend on what you say about him. Believe me, Sergeant Kenworthy, I have observed the work of your office. Anyone can see how they rely on you.'

'That's as may be. Behind it all there's a rule-book. I can't say I see much hope for Helmut Schultze in that book.'

A short silence: then she looked at him with eyes beginning to fill.

'Sergeant Kenworthy—could you not make a mistake?'

'How, a mistake?'

'Could you not report that this is a case of mistaken identity? The phone-books of Gross-Deutschland are full of Helmut Schultzes. Need this be the one who served in Minsk?'

With that driving-licence photograph on his record? But Kenworthy did not mention that. He could probably even get away with that if he wanted to. The card, one of tens of thousands with its bare-bone information, was still on his desk. He could destroy that photograph in seconds. No one in Berlin would be any the wiser. But he went on exploring.

'How would that help? You yourself wanted him arrested. In Berlin he would be spirited back by the

Russians at once.

'Things are less dangerous than they were. They grow less dangerous every week.'

'You think so? As a man of firm body, he would have to be investigated as an undischarged ex-serviceman.'

'Better that.'

'And you would be parted from him again—for months.'

'I am parted from him now. I was parted from him while he was in Minsk. For two years.'

Another silence. Then she said, 'Sergeant Kenworthy, let's not play cat and mouse. You know very well what I'm thinking of.'

'Do I?'

'We must get him to the West. There are ways and means. There is traffic nearly every night. *Über die grüne Grenze*—'

The green frontier; German romanticism was deathless. Oddly enough, it was that poetry of the self that lay at the heart of the horrors that had been committed. What sort of romantic had one to be to see a green girdle round Berlin in this winter of annihilation? There were the beginnings of a grey plain, frosted over, criss-crossed by the patrols of allies who spent most of their time sizing up each other's throats.

'And how do you reckon you'd manage that?' he asked, his tone agreeable.

'You'd hardly expect me to tell you, I'm sure—and have the ground cut from under my feet. Not that you and your friends will ever win that battle. For every gap you close, a new one will open.'

It was true: there was a regular trek of frontier traffic. Sometimes the Russians opened fire; and sometimes the British, Americans or French made an arrest.

'And when you get to the West?'

'I have my plans. Forgive me if I sit tight on them.'

She smiled—without strain, without hypocrisy. There was a close understanding between her and Kenworthy. She was confident of it.

'At least, I used to think I had plans. I'm afraid the dream's fading, thanks to your efficiency.'

He brought them back insistently to the central subject.

'Which agency would you use? Alexis? Silbernes Kreuz? Peter Fromm?'

Despite her self-control, he thought he saw a flicker in her eyes that might mean that his knowledge shook her. The point he was making was that immediate post-war Germany was as full of lost people as it was of others trying to find them: ex-internees, stragglers from forlorn battlefields, bombed-outs, wanderers, prisoners of war, men who might or might not have been killed in action. In their wake had sprung up a mushroom field of private agencies, all claiming to put their best effort into finding lost sheep: or if not finding, accounting for them. All too often they were making an income from bleeding tenuous hopes. But as the cross-indexes grew, and as they horse-traded information with each other, the success rate nowadays was not negligible. It was also rumoured that some of these agencies trafficked in something more vital than mere information: at a fee.

'Peter Fromm's the most efficient,' Kenworthy said quietly. 'But he'd cost you a packet.'

He knew Fromm, had horse-traded with him himself to the limit of permissibility, arguably beyond it. Fromm had been a young detective-constable on the Berlin Kripo, the criminal police, when war broke out, had been called up, wounded in France, had returned to the force—but had now retired to follow his own gainful pursuits. He was a man of resources: a man, even, as far as survival permitted, of integrity. It was believed, although up to now it had eluded proof, that he ran what amounted to a scheduled service across the border.

'Sergeant Kenworthy,' Anna-Maria said, 'you are being unkind. You are talking like this, as if there were hope on our horizon, while all the time you know there is none. You could give it to us—but I know that you won't.'

She came closer to him on the settee, not to try to seduce him, but to be near with a plea from the heart.

'Sergeant Kenworthy—what would you have to lose? In a few months' time you will be away from here. In a matter of weeks after that you will have forgotten us all. You work from a position of personal strength. You are one of the few Englishmen here who know what it is all about. You make a mistake; who's to know that it was ever made?'

He stood up.

'I've work to do before I go to bed.'

'You're a harder man than I took you for, Sergeant Kenworthy,'

'May I ask you a forthright question, Frau Schultze?'

'I hadn't noticed any previous diffidence.' This in the friendliest of tones.

'How many times have you prostituted yourself for the sake of your husband's advancement?'

He had not expected her to blush.

'Sergeant Kenworthy, you are using words out of all proportion to their meaning. You are speaking from the recesses of a world that is light-years removed from ours. Did you land in France on D-Day so that you could come here to moralize?'

'Not moralize, Frau Schultze—to try to disentangle motives and actions. To try to understand what might otherwise be misunderstood.'

'Prostitution—advancement. For *advancement* read *survival*. I made a man of him, Sergeant Kenworthy— and I don't mean that in the cheap sense. I took him on as a waif, abandoned by his useless, doting mother to the oblivion of a Seminary. I turned him into an officer capable of taking charge of strong men on a battlefield. I may have used devices to help us on our way, but in your moral copy-book sense they were meaningless. They were of no consequence against my love for him. That has never changed. It has not changed now.'

'Does he know how he got into the SS? Who did you have to sleep with to achieve that?'

'He never suspected. I suppose you will now go and tell him—to see what that will trigger off?'

'I think that might be counter-productive. He'd doubtless forgive you—as you forgave him for Dörli.'

'The situation was entirely different. He needed something from Dörli that I never needed in my life.'

He went towards the door. She tried a last soft-tongued appoach.

'Won't you please give us our chance, Sergeant Kenworthy? No one else can.'

The next morning he decided to close the Schultze file in the normal way, if only for the sake of administrative tidiness. He was just about to put his signature to the papers when one of the staff majors came into his office, in company with a young captain whom he did not know.

'Good morning, Sergeant Kenworthy. Anything interesting happening these days?'

He picked up the report where Kenworthy had casually laid it and began almost idly to read it. Before he reached the end of the first page, he beckoned the captain to come and read over his shoulder.

'This one seems a right bastard to me, Kenworthy.'

'A lot of them seem a bit less bastardly, when you get down to what makes them tick, sir.'

'Oh, come, Sergeant Kenworthy—not getting soft in your old age, are you?'

'I probably always was a bit soft, sir.'

'Yes: reading between your lines, I gather his wife's quite a piece,' the major said. Kenworthy held his tongue.

'No dilemma about this one, anyway. A plain case for the Russkies.'

'More's the pity, sir.'

'Why do you say that, Sergeant?'

'I've turned the man inside out. I just happen to see how it all came about. If I had my way, I'd let the Belgians or Dutch have him.'

'Is he on either of their lists?'

'No, sir. Because he was not a known character to them. But they'd be interested if they knew the details. He'd get a squarer deal from them.'

'He'll hang or be shot, whoever gets him. In any case, it's out of the question. He had a spell in Haus Ehrlich.'

'And they let him escape.'

'Precisely. To see what he'd do. To see whom he'd contact. He comes straight to us, and you can bet they know that. They'll have had tags on him ever since he landed back in Berlin. Someone high on their Wanted list, and we don't hand him back to them? How's that for the makings of an international incident? You *are* getting soft, Sergeant.'

'It's time you sent me home, then,' Kenworthy said. 'I suppose I've just seen too much of it. Europe's a network of prison camps, compounds, forced migrants, refugees. And so we perpetuate the whole issue—fresh migrants, new internees, more homeless. If I had money to invest, I'd put it into barbed wire: bigger and better cages.'

'Sergeant, I can't believe it's you talking. You—a Londoner—who came up through the campaign—'

'I know all about that, sir. I'm not talking intelligibly, not saying what I mean to say. I'm trying to say it's a pity there can't be discretion to give some people a second chance.'

'Who got a second chance in Minsk? We can't give ourselves that kind of discretion, Kenworthy. There have to be guide-lines. We have to stay within them.'

'Obviously, sir. I've finished with Schultze as per guide-lines.'

His OC was still not back. The main activities of this office were still going forward over a sergeant's *per pro* signature. The major knew that.

'So what would you do with the Schultzes, Kenworthy— given this dangerous discretion?'

'Turn them loose. Let them try to make it across the green border.'

'What's that supposed to mean?'

'It's a phrase the natives have. It means the way to the West.'

'How could that profit them? He'd need an identity.'

'Identities are on sale, sir—at a premium.'

'What influence has he?'

'He has his wife.'

'It's not on, Sergeant Kenworthy. So move things along through the machine, please. We have our difficulties with the Russians. It would be nice not to have to keep them waiting for once.'

But the next day, Kenworthy was sent for by Staff. The major was sitting with the younger officer.

'Sergeant Kenworthy—this is Captain Piper—from one of the MI's, never mind which. They're concerned at BAOR about line-crossers. They want nothing more than to put the big operators out of business. These Schultzes—do you think they would make a reasonable shot at it, given the chance?'

'I'm sure they would,' Kenworthy said, thinking of Frau Schultze.

'There could be no question of an official discharge. It would have to look like a genuine escape.'

'I can see that.'

'The Russians can hardly crib at that. It's what they did at Haus Ehrlich.'

'Yes, sir.'

'Someone would have to take the blame. It would have to be you. I wouldn't want to entrust it to anyone else in your section.'

'Sir.'

'But I'll give you my personal guarantee, Sergeant Kenworthy, that you'll get nothing worse than a severe reprimand.'

'An *admonished* wouldn't even have to go on my conduct sheet, sir.'

'You're too clever by half, Sergeant Kenworthy. Let's wait and see what sort of a mess you make of it. I'll leave the rest of your briefing to Captain Piper.'

And Piper was content to wait until the major had left them together. He was a man with an easy style, who did not mind treating a sergeant as an equal.

'You think they'll do it through Peter Fromm, do you?'

'That's my guess. That's what I'd do.'

'We've been after Fromm for three months, but we've held off him because he's obviously one of your paid informants.'

'Very accommodating of you, sir.'

'We live and let live. But Fromm's gone on too long, and these channels have got to be plugged. Do nothing until you hear from me again. It will take a day or two to get the support and reserves set up.'

Kenworthy waited a day or two and got on with other work: routine screening of civilian employees for the Control Commission; initial documentation of the gone-to-ground Nazis who continued to be brought in—all of them small fry. He also interviewed and gave provisional clearance to a High Court judge—aware of the arrogance of a twenty-four-year-old undertaking such an assignment in a language not his own. Then, suddenly he was ordered to Staff offices again.

And this was something unique: a message emanating from Exfor Rear, the administrative mammoth behind the whole of the overseas force. Sergeant Kenworthy was offered a Class B Release from the service—demobilization out of his turn—subject to his immediate return to the Metropolitan Police Force, in which he was promoted to detective-sergeant. He accepted without need for thought.

And he never afterwards did feel satisfied that he knew the truth behind this. The Met was below strength, the crime rate in London was booming; it might be that they were scouring their lists for men to bring back. On the other hand, there were powers that wouldn't hesitate to pull any string available to get him out of questioning's way once the Schultze ploy was done.

He had to go and see the major.

'You never thought of making a career with us, Sergeant?'

'No, sir.'

'We shall miss you. I have authority to offer you an immediate commission if you will stay on.'

'And for how long would that have to be?'

'Shall we say two years?'

'No, thank you, sir.'

Captain Piper was not in Berlin. Ought he to hang on until the case was resolved? The Staff answer was firm: the army said he was to go home—he must go home. He wanted to kick himself for volunteering for even an extra hour of this misery. It surpassed belief that within a day or two he would be back home with Elspeth—for good. He had a morning of medical examinations and paper-finishing. The major left Berlin for a conference.

Kenworthy made up his mind. He left a note for Piper saying that he was carrying out his agreed part of the Schultze plan on his own initiative. It would obviously be a few days, perhaps even a week or two, before the couple could make any move. He hoped he was not jumping the gun, that there would be time for the necessary follow-up to be organized.

And in the afternoon he called on Frau Schultze. Her neighbours, he knew, would be watching. She would be gaining a fine reputation, receiving occupation soldiers while her man was inside. And, God! she was actually entertaining a man when she opened the door to Kenworthy: a young signals officer who greatly resented this interruption by a ranker. Not that there was much going on to interrupt. They were not even sitting on the same article of furniture. Kenworthy looked involuntarily at the bed, and the fussy arrangement of cushions was undisturbed. Anna-Maria caught the movement of his eyes and looked back at him with self-satisfied amusement.

So what was she up to now? New less-than-official employment? A new ration ticket? A new flat, if this one were to fold up on her? She'd be lucky: things were getting more difficult in that line. It would take more than a Royal Sigs subaltern to pull that sort of string.

And what the hell? Kenworthy asked himself. Was he jealous—on his way home to Elspeth?'

'Did you want something, Sergeant?'

A right bastard; to hell with being one of his NCO's.

'I wanted to speak to Frau Schultze, sir—on duty.'

He mentioned the name of his unit, hoped that the shit wouldn't ask to see his special identity card: he'd already handed that in.

'Speak to her, then.'

'Alone, sir, if you please.'

Anna-Maria came to his rescue, went out on to the landing, pulled the door almost shut behind them.

'Yes, Sergeant?'

Apprehensive, now; he could easily have come with the

announcement of *finis*.

'I'm going home tonight,' he said. 'Demobilization. Unexpected.'

'And my husband?'

'I'm taking the big chance, Frau Schultze. He is going to escape.'

'*Escape?*'

'This evening, first dark, it has to be between six and seven—I have a train to catch—be on the corner of the Konstanzer- and Duisburger-strassen. Keep out of sight till I've gone. Hide him. I don't know how you're going to do that, but you know your Berlin. After tonight, he's all yours.'

It did not seem to have sunk in properly yet.

'You mean—?'

'I'm going. I'm not coming back. He's all yours. I give little for your chances, but take what I'm offering.'

She came up to him and repeated the gesture of gripping his arm, then stretched up and kissed him. He gave her nothing in return, walked away from her when she released him, and did not look back.

'Goodbye, Frau Schultze.'

It was the right evening for melodrama in the ruins. Kenworthy did not tell Schultze where they were going, but walked him to their rendezvous by a circuitous route. In the darkness the wreck of Charlottenburg looked like a derelict quarry. Somewhere in the middle distance a woman screamed. Women were always screaming in darkened Berlin. It gave rise to stories of rape by the Russians. A Red Army private came up to them, stumbling with drink.

'*Englische Zigaretten!*'

Kenworthy thrust a packet of Park Drive into his hand and received in exchange a crumpled fistful of German marks, which he later counted as worth over a hundred pounds. Berlin values, 1946.

He got Schultze to the street corner he had designated. There was no one about. He took Schultze by the shoulders and pushed him into what had once been a shop doorway.

'I'm going to leave you now, Schultze. You're a free man—if the term has any meaning. A guide will be here to meet you in a few minutes' time. After that, it's in the lap of whatever gods look after people like you. And don't thank me.'

Kenworthy slipped away into darkness but did not go far. Leaning against the jamb of another wrecked arch, he waited and watched. And presently out of another crumbling angle a figure emerged—and sauntered— crossing a patch of light that fell across a wall from some unbelievably occupied apartment. The gait was that of a street-walker, mincing, pausing, posing: an act, he knew, that she was mounting solely for his benefit. There was a brief reunion with a bewildered Schultze, but it was she who cut it short, knowing that this was no time for lingering in public. They passed close by Kenworthy— and out of his concern.

The train trundled all night at an agreed twelve miles an hour across the Communist-occupied plain of North Prussia. Someone had broken the window of the compartment with a carelessly swung rifle-butt; the steam heating system was out of order. The train was under armed guard, with a commandant and an adjutant. That was the way things were beginning to be on the internationally guaranteed rail-link between Berlin and Helmstedt.

In the first grey of dawn they stopped at a vast draughty railway station, an island amid flat lands. It might have been Germany or Holland. Soup-kitchens had been set up on the platform and they shuffled with their mess-tins, several hundred sleepy, frozen men. Civilization, mid-twentieth century: they might have been lost souls in some Russian symbolist epic.

And a voice bawled out over the Tannoy, an English station announcer's voice, to the last nuance of diphthong, the vulgarity made doubly comic by the distortion of the amplifiers.

'We call this station Blighty Minus One. We offer you a pint and a half of broth like your mother makes. And if you want to shit, for Christ's sake wait till you're on the move again. We have to bloody well live here.'

Thereupon the frosted window of one of the lavatories was opened by somebody still on the train. Head and shoulders leaned out and a strident Cockney voice cut across the frosty air.

'Bugger your bloody luck, chum!'

CHAPTER 10

Kenworthy looked at the well-upholstered Anna-Maria Pagendarm and marvelled that he had once wondered how far she would let him go with her. She seemed to read his thoughts.

'We have none of us grown any younger, Mr Kenworthy—but you've weathered well. Maturity suits you.'

'Thank you very much, Frau Pagendarm. And you look the perfect Protestant pastor's wife.'

'Widow.'

'Sorry. And he had tried so hard, it seems, to get in touch with me.'

'I didn't know that in time. Otherwise I'd have found a more efficient way of looking for you than he did. He wouldn't take me into his confidence. All I knew was that he was afraid of something. But it's only since that I've recognized that it was fear: fear that was driving him out of his mind. He must have been out of it, Mr Kenworthy—stealing from that store. Of course, it was protection that he wanted: and he dared talk to no one but you. But then—refusing consular help—refusing to see me at the police station—'

'I can think of good reasons why he wouldn't want to talk to the consul. I can't think why he should have turned on you.'

'What is that phrase that they use in your newspapers? The balance of his mind was disturbed. He wouldn't even recognize me in the court-room, while I was paying the fine. And when I reached the street outside, he was already gone—lost in the milling of people. But how and why did he get out in the country so fast? And who was able to follow him there?'

'When did you first notice this fear?'

'Oh, dear—I'm losing track of time already. It was after the recording session for *Crucible*—he did not have a permanent part on the programme. He only appeared occasionally. But Max Posnan was hot on expenses. He always arranged his schedules so that those flying in from abroad could get their work done in one day.'

'And what work were they doing that day?'

'I can't tell you that. He never knew till he got to the studio. Max says that the secret of the programme is its unpreparedness. Of course, he does a lot of tidying up with his tape-splicer: *gardening*, he calls it.'

'In fact the basic success of *Crucible* depends on dishonesty, you'd say?'

She laughed warmly.

'Dear Mr Kenworthy—always the moraliser. No: dishonest is too strong a term. You might as well say that a painting of the Crucifixion by a Flemish master is dishonest. Max is an entertainer whose stock-in-trade is things that have happened in the real world. It would be pretty untidy if he did not give them some artistic shape.'

'And he specializes in hypocrisy?'

'Max Posnan's public likes to see giants thrown off the bean-stalk.'

'And something happened at that last recording that caused your husband to get himself locked away from the world?'

'It looks like that. Though what it was, whom he met there, I can give you no clue.'

'Your husband, Frau Pagendarm, must have lived with more slumbering nightmares than most men of his age.'

'My husband, Mr Kenworthy, was a good man. And for the last thirty years he has done nothing but spread warm-heartedness and wisdom.'

'There is a lot that you have to tell me, Frau Pagendarm. In the present circumstances, I hesitate—'

'Mr Kenworthy, you don't have to worry. I *want* to talk about him. By talking about him, I feel as if I am bringing him back to life.'

She was, in fact, in a highly nervous condition, and her facade of self-control was costing her heavily in borrowed energies.

'*Ja*, Mr Kenworthy, you came that afternoon to my flat. And the first thing I had to do when you'd gone was to get rid of that stupid young officer who was pursuing me.'

Thirty and more years ago—and the detail was at her fingertips. Beginning where they had left off: it was as if she had waited till this day to justify her visitor in Kenworthy's eyes.

'I got rid of him without ceremony, went straight out to see Peter Fromm. We had, of course, talked previously, and he drove a very hard bargain. A square-dealing man, Mr Kenworthy—I think you had some dealing with him yourself in your Berlin days?'

'Some.'

'He asked a high price, but he was frank. He was making a fortune many times over—but the trade would not always be there. And his overheads were high. He had to buy silence and discretion in a day when it paid people to betray their neighbours. He cost me every Pfennig we had put away over the war years. Remember—we also had to buy Helmut a new life. Fromm agreed that ours was an urgent case, but we still had to wait. He had to operate with small convoys: it was like something out of a boys' adventure story. He even had to consider phases of the moon—and whatever information he could piece together about perimeter troop movements.'

Kenworthy remembered one or two of the vital bits of information he had bought from Peter Fromm. There was always a *quid pro quo*, but the terms were always unequivocal, and Fromm had never welshed on a reckoning.

'We had to wait three weeks. I had to keep Helmut stashed away in Berlin. I knew that your own section might have a hue and cry out for him. I have often wondered—'

She looked at Kenworthy through narrowed eyes.

'I knew it could be a put-up job. And Peter was so desperately afraid of that that I thought at one moment he was going to refuse to take us on. However, he just added a percentage. Oh, they were wildly unreal days. There came moments when you had to make your choice—then close your eyes and charge blindly ahead. Peter said we had to reckon with an infiltration attempt—which, he said, hardly worried him, as long as he spotted it in advance. I asked him, was he going to stage a decoy? He said no, string them along, keep them congratulating themselves. That was the way to take the sting out of infiltrators. No British counter-agent was going to have reserves to call on in the middle of the Russian zone.'

She was a woman who had, perhaps, had too much comfort in her middle years, too much whipped cream on her *Torten* in the Lutheran ladies' circles. But she had gambled in her time.

'You left me alone at that Berlin crossroads. I hoped you'd know what I meant when I minced past you. You hit me on the raw with something you said once. Prostitution, you said: but can't even that be self-sacrifice? You said I'd bought him into the SS: something had to be done to buy him into current German society. I was single-minded in Hans Jürgen's interest. Think of that as a kind of integrity.'

It seemed to matter so much to her—

'Just one more question on this issue,' Kenworthy said, 'and I promise I'll not bring it up again. Did Hans Jürgen know—ever—about that SS business?'

'No—and you must promise me that you'll never—'

She pulled herself short. Kenworthy, over the years, had observed some grotesque moments in the unreality of recent bereavement. The check brought her back cruelly.

'We were at the crossroads,' he said. 'Berlin after dark. I was turning my back on concerns such as yours for ever.'

'Your wife's still alive, Mr Kenworthy?'

'Very much so, thank God.'

'I'd like to meet her.'

'You shall.'

And that could be useful. Elspeth had a way of knowing things about women.

'I had to find somewhere for Helmut other than my flat. I had to gamble again. I had to trust someone—I, who had sworn I would never trust human beings again. I had to trust a woman I'd worked with. She didn't let me down. But it was agony, knowing him free—what a word!—and still not able, not daring, to be with him. Not being able to help him get over the four terrible weeks that he'd had in your tender care. Yes: you can smile, Mr

Kenworthy. We all knew in Berlin how docile you were. And we all knew what to expect from docility in the long run. Sometimes I think I don't know anything as frightening as kid gloves.'

'It all depends on what you think might be brought to the surface. If it happened to be Schultze of Minsk—'

'Mr Kenworthy, he was a helpless pawn in everybody's game. The NKVD wanted to know to whom he would turn if they set him at liberty. You British used him as a trap to break Peter Fromm's escape route. And you failed.'

'So he took the obvious step—and became the nation-loved *Radio Pastor*. There are one or two gaps in the story still, Frau Pagendarm.'

'I know. And I'm going to keep nothing from you.'

The movement order, when it came cryptically from Fromm, was to report to a night-club in Halensee.

Fromm was inflexible on the matter of personal property. Souvenir photographs, identity papers, currency, were to be no more than a person might be expected to carry about a day's business in the city. All West German marks had to be disposed of, if necessary jettisoned, before they left the Allied perimeter.

Halensee was chosen because there were one or two night-clubs now functioning over at the lakeside resort within the city boundaries. It was a point on which a festive party might be seen to converge, and which they could leave together, late at night, without arousing suspicion.

They met over a midnight meal-table and the disparate group began, in unpromising fashion, to get to know each other. Anna-Maria was as outgoing as ever and miraculously appeared to know the lyrics of the tendentious ditties that were sung, *chansonnier*-fashion, in the cabaret. Her personality reached across the board in an attempt to start unifying the party. But each of the travellers wanted to continue to exist in his own orbit. There was a Dr Felix Krause, a chemist whose work on plastic explosives would ultimately have made the V1 and V2 look like children's toys. He had appealed several times to the British to take him over to their camp, before the Russians came for him in the small hours. Now, in despair, he was buying his own way to freedom. He wanted to talk to no one except his wife, an unbending woman who rejected familiarity. There were two men of military age: Tradern, tall, lean and distrustful of anything that he had not himself initiated; Lerche, short, also lean, who looked as if he had lost the habit of getting anything out of life. The pair were sufficient unto each other's needs for companionship.

And finally there was Helmut: silent, supercilious towards the floorshow, ill at ease with all fellow men; and clearly disturbed by his wife's ability to sororize with anyone at any level.

The wines were expensive—and pretty poor. The food was dubious: Hamburgers at extortionate prices. Dr Krause made an effort to talk to Helmut about the hopelessness of Germany's economic recovery. Lerche began to tell Anna-Maria a tale about his personal retreat across Poland.

The evening ended with a sentimental ballad: *Sag' beim Abschied, leise Servus.* They all went through the motions of singing that. Fromm had warned them in advance that they had at least to try to look as if they were making merry. He met them after the show, disguised as a taxi-driver. But they did not ride far. He set them down in shadow and led them personally to a belt of pines, almost within sight of a British post. This, he explained, was to accommodate the studied routines of a particular regiment. Spaced-out sentries were visited regularly through the night by a roving picket. Between sentries, therefore, one might be lucky, or one might run into *force majeure*. A single sentry was emphatically not *force majeure*, and if one waited till the patrol had visited him, the safest crossing-point was in the vicinity of his post. So Fromm argued: and it worked. The Russian cordon was at its worst inefficient and at its keenest murderous. It could be predicted only by an observer in the right place at the right time. Fromm put his travellers down to cover in the No Man's belt, where they waited for an unknown scout whom he eventually sent, and who led them through a nursery plantation along wire fences, and finally along a maze of peasant tracks. Even as they were settling into the farm in which they were going to spend their next ration of daylight hours, there was a volley of rifle-shots less than a mile away. That was someone who had tried to make it without paying Fromm's fee.

They moved on again the next night, led by a local guide in the absence of Fromm, who took them along a route that confounded all sense of direction. They covered less than fifteen kilometres in all, and in direct distance they were still frighteningly near to the capital. Then, an hour and a half before the dawn, they were told to wait in a forester's clearing. The cold was bitter and snow was beginning to swirl beyond the edge of the trees, though they had some measure of protection against the worst of it. Their pilot returned after they had begun to give up hope of him. And they were taken off singly now, to separate farmsteads.

Helmut Schultze sleeping off the march on some heap of root-crops, while Anna-Maria was having it away on the side? Kenworthy dismissed the thought as merely spiteful.

The next night they came together again. Frau Dr Krause had now discarded her bourgeois clothes and looked like some peasant woman on her way to market — and, incidentally, was proving herself as tough on the trail as some of the younger pilgrims. At one farm they lived openly as if they were labourers living under the roof. They stayed here several days, during which time they saw nothing at all of Fromm.

But he appeared before they left and gave Schultze and Anna-Maria papers which, he said, they were not merely to get to know, but to make part of their being.

'And Helmut,' Anna-Maria said, 'was a man who never did anything by halves. This was the beginning of his new self: and even before we left the farm, he had mastered the facts. He was Corporal Hans Jürgen Pagendarm of the 891st Field Regiment of Artillery in the 37th Panzer-Grenadier Division, and had served as a battery surveyor on the northern wing of the assault against Russia and the later retreat. He knew which battles he was supposed to have fought in. He knew that he had been taken prisoner at Torkovitch. He had escaped shooting by a miracle at a camp on the outskirts of Vologda. He had finally got through the wire and worked his slow way across Poland and Silesia.'

And he had been born in Königsberg, in East Prussia, in the closing years of the First World War. He had no family ties. He wanted no future under Russians or red-marshalled Poles. There was a shortage of men everywhere in Western Germany. 'And that,' Anna-Maria said, 'all helped Peter Fromm to make his fortune. He had interviewed so many relatives of missing persons. The 891st Field Regiment had been obliterated down to a handful of remnants. Fromm had already sold half-a-dozen identities from the 37th Panzer-Grenadiers. "If ever you do meet anyone claiming to be from the 891st," he told Helmut, "the odds are high that he'll be someone that I have fixed up." '

'And you, Frau Pagendarm,' Kenworthy asked. 'What subtle change of extraction did you undergo?'

'Oh, I was just a *Berliner Kind'l*—that's the name of a

beer, really. I was a barmaid from East Berlin. I'd met Hans Jürgen on Gleisdreieck underground station, the day he landed from the East. We were both free of foot and fancy. We both needed a more liberal climate. We opted for the green marches.'

It was a long story, and as Anna-Maria told it, it lost some of its drama in sameness and near-repetition. A long stretch was put behind them on a barge on the Elbe. Somehow, when they cast off from a wharf near Wittenberg, Hans Jürgen became more nervous than at any other time since they had set out. It was as if the metres-wide stretches of cold ruffled water all round him had cut him off from flight.

Even the Red Army could not man every metre—or every half-mile—of a frontier that ran from the Baltic to Bohemia. They made their way, with daily scrapes, to a British post. But this time there was no attempt at evasion. They reported themselves, were held in a transit camp pending interrogation: an artillery survey corporal and, in another wing of the same cantonment, a *Berliner Kind'l*. It seemed at first as if the only paradise beyond the green marches was another grey compound.

'Where was this?' Kenworthy asked.

'In the north, between Schwerin and Lübeck.'

'And you all got through?'

'Some quicker than others—we soon saw the last of Dr Krause and spouse.'

'Don't evade the question, please, Frau Pagendarm. I said did *all* get through? I was thinking especially of the two who were presumably ex-soldiers. What were their names, again?'

'Tradern and Lerche. I had almost forgotten them. They were a strange couple. They did not want anyone's company except each other's. I mean, one day, Helmut would talk to Tradern for an hour or two, and you'd think that the ice had been broken. But then suddenly Tradern would grow silent again. We all distrusted those two. Well, everyone distrusted everyone else.'

'And what happened to them?'

'I'm afraid they got lost.'

'Lost, Frau Pagendarm?'

'Mr Kenworthy, they disappeared. We were not to ask questions. It was a habit that it was healthy to get out of.'

'They *disappeared*, Frau Pagendarm?'

'It was not long before we finally reached the West: one of those nights when it was felt safer to disperse us to several billets. When we reassembled the next morning, they didn't show up. We thought perhaps they'd lit out on their own.'

'Did you believe that, Frau Pagendarm?'

She looked at him for an instant with quizzical anxiety. His tone had become that of the professional policeman on the brink of a breakthrough.

'It is all very well, in the solid comfort of this office, Mr Kenworthy, examining comings and goings in the light of cold reason. I am talking about a lonely, winter-bound, terrifying corner of the province of Mecklenburg—'

'I know all that, Frau Pagendarm. I also know that if I were not now pressing you, you'd rather not be talking about Tradern and Lerche at all. Is that not so?'

'For a very good reason,' she said, relapsing into a thin and contrived smile. 'We'd all assumed that they were undercover men, Mr Kenworthy—*your* men. When they cut loose from us, so near to our destination, we assumed that they had gone to report.'

'They were not mine, Frau Pagendarm. By then I was home, dry and no longer interested.'

They could even have been double agents. They could have met with many kinds of accident. Or perhaps the tensions had been too much for someone's nerves on that trek across the plains.

*

So Pagendarm was held for some months while he was processed for demobilization. For the spring of 1946 he was hired out as an agricultural labourer, revelling in sunshine, fresh air and work with his limbs. He studied, too, returned to his first love—theology. Cologne, ten years ago—it seemed more like fifty—had left him embittered against Rome and the hierarchy. He had long talks with a village pastor, and with a chaplain who was working in the rehabilitation camps. Everyone thought him an excellent candidate for a Lutheran college. Anna-Maria (whom he married according to the rites of his new allegiance a week after his second ordination) had worked as a civilian, now officially approved, at one of the larger HQ's to help finance him through college. Everything was set fair for the future Radio Pastor.

CHAPTER 11

It was difficult to think of *Commander* Clingo, even with Bill looking disgustingly at home in the Commander's office. It seemed to Kenworthy that there was something a good deal less grand about that office with Bill Clingo in it.

'And you're ready to believe all this, are you, Simon?'

'Roughly,' Kenworthy said.

'To start off as a Catholic priest, and end up as a popular Protestant?'

'A priest is what he had always wanted to be.'

'Having strung up how many priests in Minsk? It doesn't add up, Simon.'

'It added up to Hans Jürgen Pagendarm.'

'There's no wonder somebody finally caught up with him.'

'Granted. And he knew at the last *Crucible* that he had been caught up with. Therefore what we want is—'

Kenworthy became as businesslike as if he had been the Commander's superior: which throughout their parallel careers had been the case.

'We want Max Posnan. We want a working script of the forthcoming *Crucible*. And we want any video-tape that exists of all sessions so far.'

Clingo laughed with badly acted mirthlessness.

'Posnan's in Sicily. It's a joke in his office: when in doubt, look for a new Mafia twist. There are never, it seems, whole working scripts for *Crucible*. There can be sudden changes of emphasis, which occur only off the cuff, when he has witnesses off their guard. The final pattern exists only in Posnan's mind. And he has taken his mind with him to the Mediterranean, along with all his key staff. There are no bits and pieces from this show lying about. Only he knows what's become of them.'

'There must have been something left over in the cutting-room. Some technician, some cameraman, some sound-recorder must know what went on.'

'There were no clips left lying about, no unscrubbed tape. We've flown a man to Palermo, and Posnan is standing firmly on the independence of the media, the confidentiality of news sources. The question arises whether *Crucible* is a news programme within the meaning of the act. And whether it's worth while testing the High Court view of that. Posnan is taking the line that he's in the same case as a reporter who would rather go to gaol than betray an informant. The popular press is solidly with him. He says that his technicians' union will support him all the way.'

'It takes more than technicians to make a programme,' Kenworthy said. 'It also takes performers. Someone must know who came to the studio that day—someone in reception, someone in cosmetics—'

Clingo preened himself with the satisfaction of a man who has not missed a trick.

'We've followed all that up. There were two Dutchmen, who've gone back to Holland. But their names and addresses were taken by Accounts Department, for forwarding their expenses. So our Dutch oppos are getting their statements, which we await with interest. There was also a retired Brigadier, who seems to have been in the hot seat about something to do with Dutch civilians during the war.

'And did this Brigadier know Pagendarm?'

'Only from *Crucible*. He had seen the man on the screen.'

'Do you mind if I take a look at this Brigadier, Bill?'

'Do anything you like, Simon. Break every rule in the book, if you want to—not that you're bound by the book any more—or ever were, for that matter. Go to any lengths you can think of, if only you can take us one little stage further.'

Which was Clingo *par excellence*, because at the first whiff of unorthodoxy, he'd be quaking in that bloody great chair.

Brigadier Devereux spent long lonely evenings at his embroidery frame, working horses and dogs on the printed patterns that he bought at the wool shop. When Kenworthy called, he was engaged on a mother and foal by a Welsh tarn.

'I hope to God I haven't to go all over it again, Kenworthy. It seems to me I've taken every Bobby in the Home Counties over every log-entry in that skirmish. That's all it was, you know: little scrap in a corner. Tidying up the field because they were getting *chokka* with the odd shell in Corps HQ.'

He went to a shelf and brought down a ring-file of military incunabula, all beautifully docketed, with sketch-maps on squared paper.

'Nijmegen's up here, off the map. Second Army's regrouping. We're swabbing up the front—if you can call it a front: islands of line regiments from a Waffen-SS division. And these self-propelled guns are giving them the belly-ache at Corps. Six of them, half a mile apart. The Isle of Elys, on our right, are told off to clobber three of them, the other three are ours. Get the situation? Now here, you see, there's a road bridge, the only one for miles around that's not mined. So my lads have to cross it, and I've yesterday's aerial photographs down from Brigade, and I can see, Mr Kenworthy, slit-trenches, in and around this copse, covering it. So we've got to pin Fritz down in them, are you with me? Two hours after dawn is our H-hour. Bit late for my habits, but let them think they're safe for another day, see? Then, five minutes before the barrage, there's panic from an RA subaltern in an observation post down in this field. Says there are civilians coming down to the bridge, led by a priest with a white flag. Priest says they're starving in St Baaf, haven't had fresh supplies in the place for three weeks. So he's bringing them through our lines.'

'Did you see this priest with your own eyes?'

'Oh, he'd tried to come to HQ the previous evening. But I had O Groups to brief, services to co-ordinate, intelligence reports to read. I'd no time. There was only one of me.'

The Brigadier, brittle, with few enough more years to run, had not lost all his energies. He was an excited talker.

'A battalion, Mr Kenworthy, numbered 1,001 men, the odd man out being the RSM. Counting replacements, I'd lost 705 since the beach-head. I had 612 left of the men I'd set out with. How many more was I going to have to throw away, so they didn't lose their afternoon nap back at Corps? It was Dunkirk all over again: men who were the salt of the earth made a sitting target, while a rabble of peasants held them down. I told the Gunner lieutenant to get back to his post, to wave the refugees back if he could, but at all costs to get his battery on target according to fire-plan.'

John Devereux's eyes saw deeply into the past.

'They can't have been starving in St Baaf, you know. They had good kitchen gardens, potato-clamps full, their own milk and eggs.'

'And the barrage was loosed off as planned?'

'To the minute. I was sorry for St Baaf: but not for my regiment.'

And Posnan had mentally scripted a one-sided version of this? With Pagendarm on the jury?

'What form did the inquisition take? At the recording session, I mean.'

'Let's have a Scotch, shall we?'

Devereux called for Hedges and the little Cockney, disapproval of such liberality expressed in every movement of his fleshless limbs, brought out a half-finished bottle of Johnnie Walker.

'I had to face the jury. After a lot of poncing about with powder-puffs, under hot bloody lights. And then they were each supposed to ask me a question. I dare say you've seen the programme.'

Kenworthy nodded.

'Always watched it myself, but I'll roast in hell before I ever do again. It was the American who opened the batting order—evangelist. Quiet chap. Always gives the impression of seeing both sides. "So you deliberately brought down a cone of fire," he said, "on thirty unarmed civilians?" "It wasn't as simple as that," I told him, and he said, "Yes, but that's what happened, though, isn't it?"

'And I went on with what I've just said to you. But of course, there's small print in the contract and *Crucible* can snip out anything they want from the tape. So I stopped short of blowing my top. Posnan was waiting for that.'

Kenworthy took a small, appreciative sip of his whisky.

'Next wicket down was the don chap from Oxford. I never went much for him. Double-tongued. Answers to match all conditions. But I thought he was fair to me. Did I consider myself *au fait*, he asked, with the laws and usages of war? And I said yes, scrupulously. And he said was I convinced, on second and third thoughts, that my decisions at St Baaf had been consonant with those usages. "Scrupulously," I said again.

'Then came this anonymous character they call the Man-in-the-Street—all common sense and platitudes. "Only one question," he said, smirking as if that in itself had been a clever thing to say. "Are you a family man, Brigadier?" "No," I said, "I am a professional warrior—or, at least, I used to be. I never thought it fair to imperil hostages of my own creation." '

'And what did the German priest ask you?'

'He asked me nothing. "No questions," he said, when his turn came. Man I've always liked, oddly enough. Makes his religion a pleasure, never a burden. But he must have been off colour that day. He looked as if he hadn't been attending to what the others were saying.'

'No,' Kenworthy said.

'You speak as if you have inside knowledge.'

'Up to a point. You've been lucky, Brigadier. It's needed murder to take that edition of *Crucible* off the air, You'd have come off badly.'

'Hedges told me to leave it alone. He has an uncanny knack of knowing.'

'Tell me one thing: the Dutchmen were also scheduled for the same session. Did you come across them?'

'No. Witnesses in *Crucible* are kept strictly apart. Like a law court.'

'You've been lucky. But it wasn't you that friend

Posnan was gunning for.'

'No?'

'You'd have made fair game as a curtain-raiser. The audience would have thought at first that you were the main victim. That was to prepare them for the big shock to come. Will you lend me Hedges for a few minutes?'

'Help yourself. You will find he is very proud of his trivial little mind. Want me to sit in?'

'Better not.'

The rapport between Kenworthy and the Brigadier was as near as nothing perfect.

CHAPTER 12

Hedges was sitting in his shirt-sleeves at the kitchen table, managing a perplexity of cabalistic signs in tables neatly ruled on cheap writing paper. Kenworthy looked knowingly over his shoulder.

'I see Traction in the two o'clock is your banker.'

'The Brigadier wants Alicante.'

'He could be proved right, of course.'

'That'll be the bloody day.'

'Was he right at St Baaf, do you think?'

'Not my business, Mr Kenworthy. My job was to see that if he bought it, he died with his boots boned. I drove him about in his battle-wagon, and left the mistakes strictly to him.'

'And knew when to lose your way, I'll be bound.'

'We're both still here, Mr Kenworthy.'

'If my name were Posnan, it's you I'd have wanted on *Crucible*.'

'He did: but not this child.'

'Were you frightened of anything in particular?'

'Yes: Posnan.'

'I mean of something particular that might have come to light.'

'No comment.'

'You mean, from what you've been able to gather from the Brigadier's account of this interview, Posnan missed his main chance after all?'

'No comment.'

'Don't you realize, Hedges, that that silly phrase is one of the most deadly confessions in the business?'

'No comment.'

'Let's try another way round, then. Will you play a little game with me, Hedges?'

'It strikes me it's you who are playing all the games, Mr Kenworthy.'

'As long as you know. Let's pretend that I'm Posnan, and that by some bribe or miracle I've got you on the programme.'

'A thousand a week for life. Sterling and cash.'

'We all have our price. Mr Hedges—would you describe yourself as close to your employer?'

'Not as close as he is, the mean old sod.'

'Ha-ha. And you were with him in Holland?'

'Button-stick at the ready.'

'How beautifully put. Would you describe the Brigadier as a betting man, Mr Hedges?'

'It's been known.'

'Did he lay any bets in Holland, as far as you know?'

'I'm not answering that.'

'Well, let's be grateful for a change in phraseology.'

'I'm still not answering.'

'You don't have to. You already have. What was the stake? It was with the Commanding Officer of the Elys, wasn't it? Your sister battalion in the brigade, operating on your flank?'

Hedges resigned himself to letting it out before it was squeezed from him piecemeal and painfully.

'Colonel Devereux, Brigadier as he is now, had a Humber Snipe staff car, modified, privately and against all the rules, by his brother-in-law in REME. He had a fold-away bar, a wash-basin, refrigerated drinks cupboard. Every CO in the division was jealous of it. He bet Crawford—that's the Elys' CO—his staff car against an ordinary one, that he'd have all his objectives that day before the Elys had theirs.'

'So you might say he put down a bombardment on thirty civilians for the sake of winning a bet—for the sake of not losing a staff car? Or, let's put it another way: that's what Posnan was going to say.'

'Christ Almighty.'

'Yes, Hedges,' Kenworthy said.

Kenworthy went back to Devereux.

'A narrow escape, Brigadier. Were you listening? I left the door open on purpose.'

'I heard. And do you think, other things being equal, I'd have let that bet influence me?'

'I think the verdict would have been left in mid-air, Posnan fashion. It would have done you no good. But I still think you were only a side-show. You know how Posnan likes to pull the big surprise. This was going to be the biggest ever.'

'I don't follow your reasoning.'

'Because I have information that you haven't. And I don't think the most daring detective-writer in print has ever tried one in which the real villain was sitting on the jury. Pagendarm appears on the programme as a paragon of Teutonic morality. And now Posnan has the chance to explode him in public. One of those Dutchmen was going to identify him.'

'You have lost me irrevocably, Kenworthy.'

'I know. It's not fair. I am thinking aloud. And coming to the conclusion that there may be someone we don't know about yet, behind Posnan's scripting.'

'I'm afraid I can't help you there.'

'No, you can't. But I may call on you again later.'

'By all means. Good for anything honest, you know.'

'I don't need to be told that.'

'Let's see if Hedges is sitting on any more Scotch, shall we?'

CHAPTER 13

Kenworthy was bored by detection procedures. Even at the height of his career, they had interested him less than motive. But motive was never admissible evidence. It was an indicator, that was all.

The field work had fallen to a Superintendent Mitchell, who had been known, though not well, to Kenworthy four years ago as an Inspector. Mitchells' files—and the assembled contributions of his teams— were difficult to fault. Pagendarm had been dismissed by the court in London at about ten thirty in the morning on a Thursday. He had been found dead in a Chiltern hamlet on the Friday morning. The pathologist put death as at the earliest about three p.m. on the Thursday, at the latest dawn on the Friday. The weapon was a miniature automatic and had been fired at a range at which even a Noddy-gun like that could not have missed. There was no trace of the gun, but it would have been so easy to dispose of it that only a stroke of luck was likely to find it.

Pagendarm's body had minor scratches, attributable to blackberries and wild briars, made not long before death. There were no indications that the killing might have taken place other than where the body was found.

How had the murdered man got from Marlborough Street to the rural by-ways of Hertfordshire, and why?

The favoured explanation was that he had been forced into a car within half a minute of leaving the court, but there was no bystander evidence to support this. Since there were no traces of struggle near where the body was found—behind a boarding kennels, whose inmates had not been reported as making a fuss—the inference was that Pagendarm had gone there voluntarily and, by extension of argument, that he must have done so in company with someone of whom he was not afraid.

Kenworthy was never happy with early inferences: they inhibited flexible use of the imagination. He feared extensions of argument even more: they sometimes led one past vital intersections. He went himself to Marlborough Street, and at the time at which the Pastor had been released from the precincts, he set out to walk eastwards.

Going was slow on the pavement. There was an adverse crowd, several abreast in either direction. The easiest thing in the world, with luck, to lose a pursuer; but then also the easiest thing, with luck, to stay on the trail. That side of things was unpredictable. The actual skill of sleuthing was at a discount. It all depended on the arbitrary jostling of people. Then, on a pavement corner, Kenworthy saw the placard, and in a side-street a couple of coaches parked: daily, 11 and 2.30, guided tour, the City and Westminster. Mondays and Wednesdays, Oxford; Tuesdays and Fridays, Cambridge. Thursdays: Merrie England: The Cotswolds and Chilterns: lunch and dinner in Olde Englishe Tavernes.

The office was manned by a badly manufactured blonde who answered questions without natural grace. How could she be expected to remember who was on the Merrie England coach one day last week? They didn't have a passenger-manifest: this wasn't an airline. There could be half-a-dozen assorted Arabs, a gaggle of Lancashire girls, ten Germans, six Dutchmen, two

American couples and a handful of witch-doctors in their night-shirts.

'Very good for the balance of trade, I'm sure,' Kenworthy said. 'And when can I talk to the man who piloted the Tudor revellers last Thursday?'

She looked blank. He tried again.

'I'd like a few minutes with last Thursday's Merrie England driver.'

'You'll be lucky. He knocked off for his holidays last Friday evening. Gone to Torremolinos. On a coach-tour.'

'Was anyone other than he involved in boarding last Thursday's passengers?'

Evidently not — if she understood the question at all. It was hard work, but he did manage to establish a certain lackadaisical chain of facts and possibilities. The Merrie England run was not an established success, and was probably coming off at the end of this season. The takings were healthier than average if the coach was more than two-thirds full. The highlights were lunch at a mock Tudor road-house almost as soon as the green fields of the A40 were reached; a halt at a *kitsch* pottery in the hills above High Wycombe; afternoon tea among the brass warming-pans of a converted rectory in Bucking-hamshire, and dinner under the concrete Elizabethan beams of a 1950ish motel in Hertfordshire. It attracted sporadic American enthusiasm, but for the most part depended on English provincials and such groups of Italians, Scandinavians, Iberians and Aussies as were desperate to sit down at the moment when the placard caught their eye.

No: the woman at the desk was clueless as to who might have been on any particular tour. She was not in the habit of looking at them as she issued their tickets. But what, Kenworthy asked, if someone didn't come to her for a ticket? Suppose someone happened along the pavement as the coach was about to start up — and just climbed aboard. Could he get a ticket from the driver? The blonde sniggered. He could, but he wouldn't. He'd get a ride that wouldn't go through the books. The driver would pocket the fare.

Kenworthy rang Bill Clingo, who passed it down to Mitchell, who asked Thames Valley to have a look at it. One of their midday pairs fancied a snack at the *Postilion* on the A40.

But you couldn't expect anybody to remember individual guests, could you or even individual days? Unless somebody broke something, or made a spectacularly outrageous complaint. Merrie England—that mob? Scampi in the basket, mostly, and Americans who wanted their beer at sub-arctic temperatures. Last Thursday? No: nothing special. What was special about last Thursday? Takings down again, and there was going to have to be a new percentage agreement with the operator if he couldn't do better than that.

Then somebody did remember something. The girl in reception, who was difficult to dislodge from what seemed a permanent telephone conversation with someone who was bringing her only disbelief and displeasure, remembered that there had been a contretemps last Thursday. The driver of the Merrie England coach, having got his party aboard and ready for the off, already half an hour behind his time-table, had come back in again, putting his head into every bar and the Gents and complaining that he was two missing. Would she go into the Ladies for him and see if anyone had died in there? No, of course he couldn't bloody well describe them to her. He knew he was two down on numbers, but they might have been Bedouins or Welsh miners for all he knew. The pub was now emptying. He waited five minutes, then drove off for the *kitsch* shop.

The *Postilion* was within easy walking distance from the spot where Pagendarm's body had been found. Had the German, emerging from the court, seen a familiar and unsympathetic person waiting for him, plunged into the crowd, seen the coach standing and clambered aboard—only to be joined by his pursuer?

Mitchell began to think he was on the road at last.

CHAPTER 14

Some bright lad in the collator's office, unknown to Kenworthy even by name, had produced a file on Pagendarm.

PAGENDARM; Hans Jürgen, *b.* 8 April 1917, Königsberg, only son of Hans Ludwig Pagendarm (killed 1918, le Quesnoy) and Olga Charlotte, *née* Illing. Educated Grothius Gymnasium, Abitur 1935, Enrolled University of Berlin, philosophy. Military service, 1935-7; commenced studies, Berlin, 1937; recalled colours 1938: 891st Fd Artillery, 37 Pz-Gren Div, employed battery survey; Belgium, France, 1940; Ostfront, 1941-2; PW Russia, East Poland, 1943; escaped Berlin, 1946; Coll Theo Kassel, 1947. Ordained, Reformkirche, Hesse-Nassau, 1949. *M.* Anna-Maria Kummerfeld, same year. Pastorates in Ibbenbüren, Dithmarsch and Rendsburg, 1949-54. Priest-in-charge, Braunfeld a.d. Aller, 1954-present. Broadcaster and Journalist. Pubs: *Nails in the Door*, 51; *Rome and the Jews in the aftermath of the Hundred Years War*, 52; *New Neighbours*, 55; *The Church and the Media* (pamphlet, 57); *Jesus Christ, Freedom Fighter*, 61; *Without Martyrdom*, 64; *Crusader in the Hearth*, 65. Hobbies: Talking and listening.

The collator had added a note: *interesting progression in*

his literary ambition, from early academic to journalistic opportunism. And, Kenworthy added to himself, note proselytizing zeal of new convert.

Next came an aide-memoire of an interview with the official from the consulate who had visited Pagendarm in cells:

From Klaus Kullin, Under-counsellor:
Visited subject on receipt of notice from Metropolitan Police. Found Pagendarm sullen to the point of autistic. He obstinately refused bail and represen-tation, though I watched proceedings as matter of course. Pagendarm gives impression of having succumbed to a moment of temptation which has left him temporarily (?permanently) reluctant to look the world in the eye. He has a weighty middle-class following at home which will be dissipated when this hits the headlines; also a caucus of opponents (leftists, atheists, and disruptives) whose blades will now be drawn for the kill.
Collator's Note: Last infelicitous phrase recorded before P's death known.
The Under-counsellor added that he was not himself a Pagendarm fan. He had heard his broadcasts occasionally when on home leave. He admired his technique: P had a common-sense manner of cutting through what were problems to some. But there was nothing sparklingly new in what he had to say, rather a facility for making it sound original. He had a journalistic flair for spotting tomorrow's popular copy, a feeling for topicality. Witness the lessons that he had drawn for home consumption from the terrorism at the Munich Olympics. He could write an epistle, without apparent trivialization, on the outcome of a World Cup match. His thoughts on the first lunar promenade had inspired many.

There followed other assessments, from random commentators drawn upon as London opportunities offered.

From Kurt Heining, 22, research student (solid state electronics), Ealing Technical College:
Obviously I don't listen to him when I'm not at home, and not then if I can help it. But that's not easy because my parents are both bemused by him, and it's silence in the house when Opa Pagendarm's holding forth.

What I can't stand is his complacency. It's all so facile. He's good at finding the right phrase. He says what people like my parents want to think, but thinks of it before they do.

From Hilde Backnang, 19, girl-friend of the above, student at Regent Street School of Languages.
I could get hooked on him easily. Not that I'd ever stay in to listen to him, but if I'm about I'll switch him on. What appeals to me is that he likes people for what they are, not for what he thinks they ought to be. He's not like any other parson I've met, Protestant or otherwise.

He does a lot for people, too. I've a friend at home who wrote to him after one of his broadcasts. She was shacked up with a man whom she couldn't take home because he'd have insisted on sleeping with her and her parents would have been horrified. He wrote back, personally, within a week, two pages of it. And when she'd read them, there just didn't seem to be a problem.

From Dr Georg Fischer, Lektor in Contemporary German Studies, University of London.
Pagendarm has a formidable following, not just because he is the apotheosis of common sense. He has the art of making people think it is their own common sense that they are discovering. He presents religion as

a joyful, not a miserable thing, rejects the embracing of austere disciplines for their own sake, says life is to be lived, and that the codes that make that possible for a true Christian need not be prohibitive. Faith, service and salvation can be achieved without martyrdom: he did a short book along those lines in the 1960's and it ran through several printings in paperback. A man can choose the way of the Cross for himself, he says, but he has no right to prescribe it for others. Anathema to Pagendarm is the man who makes life misery for his wife or dependants in the name of some creed whose standing orders are man-made.

He is a popular man because he knows how to be: an astute master of herd psychology. Added to which he has a rich voice, soporific or challenging to meet the occasion, pleasant features, eyes that an honest man is apt to judge honest, and a smile that is personal to the observer.

Of course, he has only to make one bad mistake in public to undermine his long years of build-up. But his God (or his gods) have been on his side so far.

From Gerhard Löschke, visiting preacher at the London Reformkirche.
I knew Pagendarm when we were both ordinands in Kassel, just after the war. But I can't say I knew him well. He wasn't in my set, in fact I can't remember that he belonged to any particular set. He was rather a morose individual, not an uncommon trait in ex-servicemen indulging in a few months of the contemplative life. I am surprised at the turn that his life has taken. No one who knew him at Kassel would have forecast today's popular figure. But here we are back at the German ex-soldier. Pagendarm is not the only one to have needed hibernation before re-awakening. See an early story by Heinrich Böll called *Onkel Fred.*

Pagendarm may have been helped by coincidence. In the late 'fifties, the churches were beginning to see the need to stay abreast of new developments in communications. Pagendarm himself contributed a pamphlet on the subject, largely for vocational consumption. Early television appearances by priests had been amateurish, sometimes farcical. A new professionalism was needed. The church began to run training courses, produced a cadre of pastors who were to be regarded as a panel of specialists. Pagendarm qualified brilliantly, stole the stardom of a weekly Lutheran Half Hour. He had all the touches.

It would not be true to say that the church has remained totally with Pagendarm. There are many who feel that he spends longer hours in the studio than he does in his parish—that something is going unattended-to: that much that is basic is being omitted from the Gospel according to Pagendarm. There are rumours that he has been sent for and talked to more than once, after which he made three or four consecutive broadcasts in which sectarian considerations, dragged in by the scruff of their necks, almost put the thing on to two simultaneous and imcompatible planes. It would not surprise me if Pagendarm and the organized church eventually part company.

From Heinrich Vick, on remand for possession of cannabis.
I listened to the bastard once. Pass your professional efficiency bar. Get a house with a car-port and a mortgage within your income and Jesus will love you.

There followed a lengthy article, clipped from a glossy women's magazine, *Haus und Hüterin*, a cheesecake profile of Anna-Maria which did more to popularize certain consumer goods than to say anything fundamental about the woman herself. There were spectacular photographs of Anna-Maria turning an omelette in her work-saving kitchen; Anna-Maria bending with a miniature, mint-condition trowel to her herb garden; Anna-Maria at her reproduction Biedermeier writing-desk: *often the Pastor's wife takes pen in hand to offer unsolicited consolation to her husband's most poignant correspondents.*

Pagendarm did not appear in the article except as an absent but unquestioned eminence. There was a picture of Anna-Maria folding one of his boldly floral-patterned shirts on the eve of a holiday in Corfu. *There is hardly a moment for relaxation in the sixteen-hour day of the Pastor whose parish is the air. But once a year the Pagendarms frankly escape. And, frankly, they do not stint themselves. This year it is to be Marbella. For next year their minds are not yet made up—but Frau Anna-Maria says wistfully that one of these days they would love to return incognito to the scene of childhood memories on the quiet Baltic coast.*

The magazine was three months old, and the last item on the file was a letter to its editor, published a week later:

How much longer, one wonders, can the all-things-to-all-men brigade continue to get away with it? Pastor Pagendarm knows all the answers to those questions he chooses to deal with. Your insight into his domestic circumstances is a splendid advertisement for the rewards of his skilfully presented virtue. One wonders what might have happened if by some time-quirk John the Baptist had restricted his propaganda to Wiesbaden and Biarritz in the 1890's.

CHAPTER 15

It had been put to Anna-Maria that it would be helpful if she could hold herself in London for a few days longer at the disposal, if he needed her, of Superintendent Mitchell. She agreed more readily than he had feared that she might. It was only a hole in her life, she told Kenworthy, that yawned for her now in the home that *Haus und Hüterin* had made such a splash of. She was racking her brain even now for some way to dispose of the lot without ever having to set foot in the place again.

Solitude was Anna-Maria's greatest enemy. But given human society, she made the necessary effort at once. Kenworthy kept his promise to take her to his home, and she began looking outward at once on the journey through the suburbs.

She and Elspeth eyed each other like a couple of wrestlers in the first hand-grip who, unbeknown to the ringside seats, have in a leisurely three seconds contemplated and rejected a variety of opening gambits. It was a clean autumn morning, crisp and enlivening. Elspeth had a few tea-cloths and aprons to go on the line. Anna-Maria looked perfunctorily at the autumn litter of the herbaceous borders. Could such a home ever have meant anything to her?

Then the phone rang, and they wanted Kenworthy at a conference in Victoria Street. Elspeth grimaced, behind Kenworthy's back, that she was sure that that had been fixed. Kenworthy assured her by esoteric signal that it had not. But he was glad; there had been times before, when Elspeth had been looking someone over for him, that they had only got in each other's way.

★

Bill Clingo took the chair, acting the easy-going *primus inter pares* for Kenworthy's benefit. But there was an underlying rubbing-of-it-in that this chair had never been Kenworthy's. There was even a corny little speech before the agenda proper.

'Sure we're grateful to former colleague for coming out of his retreat. Valuable information about past history. Grateful if you'd continue to sit in, Simon, in case distant bells raise any echoes.'

Which Clingo clearly did not believe would happen. And if Kenworthy spoke up now and said he'd rather piss off out of it, it would take a weight off Clingo. Clingo couldn't bear being seen through.

'So down to the hard slog, gentlemen. Alibis. Matthew, what have the Dutch sent us?'

A Chief Inspector had his brief ready. It was long, it left out no detail and it was authenticated by the rubber stamp of the Gelderland police.

Two Dutchmen, Jakob Raaijmaaker, 39, present Burgomaster of St Baaf, and Piet Hanfstängl, who had been one of four children to escape with their lives from Devereux's bombardment, had been dug out by the *Crucible* team. They contributed a gory account, mostly by now local folklore, of events when a Dutch priest, passing through their village, had persuaded people to make a bid for welfare and safety under a white-flag pilgrimage. There had been one or two 'refugees' in the party whom the village could not account for. Otherwise, there was nothing new. There had been no confrontation between them and either Devereux or Pagendarm at the recording session. While Pagendarm was being fined and murdered, they were doing the changing of the guard, St James's Park and a dirty cinema in Soho.

'We'll have to accept that for the time being. Frau Pagendarm?'

'Has been in the best of company today—and still is.'

Clingo looked benignly at Kenworthy, and the general chuckle was not hostile.

'Nothing more about her alibi?'

'There can't be. About all one can say in its favour is its sheer probability. She paid the fine, moved up the court-room to intercept her husband, was frustrated by a gang-way conversation between solicitors. She saw his head seventy yards ahead of her when she reached the pavement, but kept losing it among the other heads. She saw the Merrie England coach, walked right past it, never thinking for an instant that he might be on it. Spent the afternoon in and out of department stores, took side-streets to get away from the crowd, got lost, found, lost again, turned up at the Yard, was handled at the desk, went back to her hotel to wait. We can't bust it; there's nothing to bust.'

'She bought nothing? No receipts?'

'Frankly, sir, I'd be more suspicious if she did try to produce something. I'm inclined to believe her.'

'Does she think that she was the one that he was running away from?'

'She wonders. He had rejected her when she tried to visit him in custody. She puts that down to his sense of shame.'

'Is she the sort of woman who'd carry a bijou auto-matic?'

'Who's to say?'

'Kenworthy?'

Somewhere about her person—sometimes in the lining of her coat—almost the whole of her adult life?

'I don't know,' Kenworthy said.

'But on probability?'

'On probability? Yes. No.'

'You give us a generous choice. But you are prejudiced, Simon.'

'I don't think so.'

He was objectively surprised at how rattled he felt; and self-knowledge did not make him any the less rattled.

'Oh, come, come. She must have been a very different proposition in January 'forty-six from what she is now. On your own showing, you saw a lot of her—were prepared to take risks. Be honest with us, Simon—she was the goods wasn't she?'

And Clingo exchanged glances with one or two down the table. So there'd been that sort of talk behind his back, had there? Kenworthy knew he ought not be surprised. He was being bloody childish to resent it. He had come into this determined that he wasn't going to start anything with Clingo. He wasn't going to start anything with Clingo now. But by God, he hardly thought it possible for a mature man to resent another as he resented Clingo.

Clingo moved on.

'Posnan. We continue to play low profile. He can't stay away for ever. Decision whether to try to force his hand is now with the Home Secretary. If we have to wait for the courts, we shall have to wait a long time. What have you turned up, Walter?'

A bored young inspector took his turn; he looked more like a drug addict.

'You wanted main desk callers at the TV studios. I had to lay a tart from reception to get a look at the register.'

'Was she good value?'

'I switched the bloody light off. Anyway, the list's on the table. And the names that interest us are Peter Fromm and Dr Felix Krause.'

Clingo looked at Kenworthy with self-satisfaction. There was of course nothing in this morning's information that was new to the Commander. The object of this get-together was cross-pollination.

'Two names with which we're familiar, Simon. Both of

them were with Pagendarm's party when they crossed the green frontier.'

'That's correct.'

'So what's your reaction?'

Kenworthy was in no mood to admire the drawing of rabbits from Clingo's hat.

'It's obvious,' he said, 'that Posnan bought his information from someone. It could be Fromm, though that would surprise me. I don't know anything at all about Krause.'

'Now a naturalized British subject. Armaments chemist, works at a Rocket Propulsion Establishment in Bucks.'

'You can talk to them. Perhaps have talked to them. But neither of them could possibly have told Posnan about Devereux. It's Posnan you need to talk to.'

Clingo laughed.

'As I said just now, that's become almost a constitutional issue.'

'I'd be happy on your behalf,' Kenworthy said, 'to undertake an expense-covered journey to Sicily.'

'So would each and any of us. Not on, Simon.'

'Let me go as a private individual, then.'

'Out of the question.'

'You'll not get a yard further forward without Posnan.'

'We shall have to.'

'I could get him here in two shakes. Give me his address and pay for a Telex.'

'No, Simon. I've told you. Posnan is in political hands. He means trouble, real trouble.'

Whereupon Kenworthy said no more. But when the meeting was over, he got Posnan's whereabouts within a quarter of an hour, simply by flattery on the phone of a young collator whom he rang up to congratulate on the Pagendarm dossier.

Then he sent his Telex.

*

Anna-Maria had gone when Kenworthy reached home. Elspeth had set her on her route to the West End, where she was dining with friends from the London German church.

'Well?'

'Simon—were you ever in love with Anna-Maria? Tell me honestly.'

'Never—not quite.'

'Just infatuated?'

'Not even that. Uniquely fascinated.'

'You could have had her if you'd wanted to.'

'And I didn't. I told you that thirty-six years ago.'

'I know. I'd have known if you had, whatever you told me. But the risks you took for her! You could have been court-martialled. Were you insane?'

'I think not. I think I can account for it. Berlin, 'forty-five, 'forty-six, wasn't perhaps the lowest the world ever sank to. But it was the lowest that I'd ever seen. I lived in it and with it, was of it, for six weary months. The Schultzes gave me the chance to make something decent happen to somebody: to make someone believe, myself too, that decent things could still happen to people. I think it would even have helped if I'd known for certain that they didn't deserve it. I wanted to restore somebody's confidence—and thereby my own. What did you make of her?'

Elspeth kept him waiting for her answer.

'I'd like to like her—but I'm afraid to.'

'Why's that?'

'Because I'm far from convinced that she didn't kill her husband.'

'She's devoted her whole life to loving him.'

'Granted. But all the same—'

'We shall see. I've sent Posnan a Telex. Like to see what I've told him?'

He produced the slip on which he had drafted it.

OFFER CHANCE SOLVE PAGENDARM MURDER PUBLICLY
ON CRUCIBLE KENWORTHY RETIRED YARD.

CHAPTER 16

Posnan was a casual man in a sweat shirt (*Hackensack
Tigers*) with rope-soles that looked as if he had salvaged
them from one of those Mediterranean beaches that is
used as a municipal tip. His hair was tarred rope-end.
And he received Kenworthy in a Sunday supplement
riverside villa at Staines: a safe house, lent by a friend.
Kenworthy could easily have found out who. He didn't
bother.

'I hope I'm not here for nothing, Kenworthy. And in
case that's your purpose in life, I'm revealing no sources.'

'You don't have to. I know them. At least I know the
one that matters.'

Posnan looked irritated at the attempt to stage drama.
He did too much of that himself.

'Let's have it, Kenworthy. I need to know how long to
stay. I'm missing the sunshine.'

'At first I thought perhaps it was Jewish money.'

Beneath the cultivated grossness, Posnan had sensitive
eyes.

'But as far as I know, there are no Jews to avenge in
Schultze's case.'

'So?'

'And it isn't Peter Fromm. I was negotiating with
Fromm at a time when neither of us dared drop a point.
He was in the most lucrative—and most suicidal—racket
of the century. And he didn't commit suicide. He avoided
self-destruction by steering clear of blackmail. Do you

follow me? His bargains were straight — with some of the nastiest men in creation.'

'It wasn't Fromm,' Posnan said. 'I tried to get Fromm to play, tried to bring him into this, because he's the best private eye on the continent. He came over to see what it was about, but he wouldn't touch it at any price.'

'So it has to have been Krause.'

Posnan did not react.

'Whose only contact with Schultze, as far as I know, was when Fromm worked them over the border: together with two Germans called Lerche and Tradern, whom they suspected of being British moles.'

Without actually yawning, Posnan looked bored.

'So what happened on that frontier-crossing that makes Pagendarm get himself arrested, on sight of Krause in your studio? May I say that I'm sure Krause didn't kill him, because Krause is too nicely set up in our own scientific civil service to go about playing kids' games like that —'

Posnan suddenly shifted his posture.

'You jump big gaps, Kenworthy. I'll tell you about Krause. As you say, his rockets are our rockets now. Krause wouldn't kill Schultze — but he couldn't stand the man. By nineteen forty-five Krause was no Nazi. I doubt whether he'd ever been much of a Nazi, and certainly not in the last years of the war. The other two Germans you spoke of — Lerche and Tradern — they gave out not to have been Nazis either. They and Krause shared common opinions. And then they discovered that Schultze had been SS. They saw him stripped at the tub in some barn, and under his armpit he had the special tattoo with which SS were branded with their blood-groups. They all disliked him. He was not a companionable man on that trip. In a way, he symbolized what had gone wrong with their nation. It helped to unify those three in their tribulations, recognizing Schultze as filth.'

'So why has it taken all these years to come to fruition?'

'Because once Krause got out and got his expertise recognized, he no longer cared. And the other two got lost somehow—as men do get lost on excursions like that. Krause as good as forgot Schultze—wouldn't have recognized him, anyway. But he did recognize Schultze's wife: in a schmaltzy article, in a weekly illustrated, a month or two ago. It disgusted him. He abominated this Radio Pastor figure—but had never connected him with Schultze. Now he knew. So he came to me to tell the tale.'

'But that didn't put you on to Devereux, did it?'

'That's only marginally significant,' Posnan said.

'I've spent most of my life dodging about in the margin.'

'I was already on to the Devereux story. Let's say that was one I got lucky with.'

Posnan rolled himself a cigarette: French papers, a blue packet of Gauloise, full caporal.

'It's your turn now, Kenworthy. What's the new story-line?'

'I'm not ready with it yet.'

'Stalling, are you?'

'No. We can only do it together. You were going to turn the tables on Pagendarm. Had he spotted that? Had somebody told him?'

'No.'

Posnan was clearly thinking hard on his own account now.

'No. Because I hadn't even decided in my own mind exactly how I was going to work it out. I was playing it by ear. There was a lot that still needed thinking through. That's one of the reasons I tried to get Fromm in on it. I might have known he'd clam up.'

He crumpled up two-thirds of his cigarette in the ashtray.

'By the way, Kenworthy, if *you're* a mole—'

Kenworthy looked at him in accusative silence for some seconds.

'I suppose we have this to go through. Somebody's got to take someone at his face value sooner or later, Posnan, even if it means performing an act of faith. I'll be honest with you. I want to get there before a man called Clingo does.'

Posnan laughed. 'I've met Clingo. So that rings truer than anything I've heard for several weeks. All right. There was something. Try as you may to keep people apart, there's limited space in a studio, and limited time to a session. I didn't want Pagendarm, Krause and Fromm to come together: but an accident happened. They caught sight of each other. And all three of them were too smart and experienced to start anything. Coldly polite: three compatriots, meeting as strangers. At least, Pagendarm and Fromm might have been entitled to know each other. From what I saw of it, Krause didn't publicly recognize Pagendarm, and Pagendarm didn't give himself away. It wasn't the encounter itself that unsettled Pagendarm. It was something that Fromm said to him, oh, a good ten minutes after their first meeting. I saw it happen. They were chatting inconsequentially in a corner—and Pagendarm suddenly went black. I know that is corny, but that's just what happened. I called for the jury-box sequence, and Pagendarm had gone to pieces. When he was asked to question the Brigadier, he couldn't bring his mind to it at all.'

'That's what the Brigadier told me.'

Posnan brought out a tatty diary from the back pocket of his jeans and looked up a telephone number.

'You say Fromm isn't a blackmailer. Well, I'm bloody everything. I'm going to promise Fromm a sub-poena in a British court if he doesn't tell me what he said to upset Schultze.'

It was a long telephone call, and Posnan was silent for

long stretches. When he put the receiver down, he was
looking satisfied.

'I take my hat off to you, Kenworthy. You got me back
from the Med to find that out for you.'

'To find out for both of us.'

'What are your former colleagues actually doing,
Kenworthy?'

'Faffing about.'

'There's no point in doing this on *Crucible* unless we
can be sure of getting there before them. Otherwise it's
sub judice and we're scuppered.'

'I know nothing about your technical side. How fast
can you work?'

'If I couldn't work at least as fast as the news boys, I'd
be out of business.'

'You haven't told me what Fromm said.'

'Fromm remembers the moment perfectly. It had him
worried at the time.'

'What did he say?'

'Fromm boobed. He's spent a lifetime of evasions, a
lifetime of lies. Sooner or later that sort of man says
something to someone that he thinks that that person
already knows.'

'You mean to Pagendarm—about Anna-Maria?'

'Very smart of you, Kenworthy.'

'But not smart enough.'

'They were taking leave of each other, actually, when I
called Pagendarm on to the set. And Fromm, off his
guard, said, "Well, give my love to Anna-Maria. And tell
her she's come a long way since the Hardtstrasse." '

'That's beyond me, I'm afraid.'

'It was beyond me, too. Peter had to expound. It was
meaningful enough to anyone who'd lived in Cologne in
the early 'thirties. The Hardtstrasse was the original
offices of the Gestapo, in the very beginning, before
things got properly organized. The implication, Fromm

says, that Pagendarm picked up like a shilling out of soot, was that Anna-Maria had been on their pay-roll even before she got to know him.'

'So that when she picked him up at the altar, she was on an assignment?'

'What do you know, Kenworthy?'

So Kenworthy told him all that he did know.

'The longer I work at this job,' Posnan said, 'the readier I am to believe anything. Even the truth.'

'Tell me this, Posnan—when you booked Pagendarm on to your jury in the first place—were you lying in wait for just something like this?'

Posnan shook his head—and Kenworthy did not doubt the smile of sincerity.

'No. He helped my international balance, and I was glad of his experience in the medium.'

And then he smiled more broadly.

'Besides, he was so anxious to buy his way on to the English air that I was able to bate his fee. Every little helps. The English public, of course, accepted him—but there's been no enthusiasm to give him a show of his own.'

'There are too many questions, Posnan, that we need Pagendarm to answer for us. Did he really go half a century, not knowing what his wife had done to him? My God, there's no wonder she had access to big enough beds to get him into the SS. Yet I'll swear that she loved him, within the meaning of the act. Though what was she up to for two years while he was in Russia? Did she get him sent there? Or did she eventually succeed in having him brought back? One thing's for sure: he went to pieces on your last session. Was his seduction from Rome no more than a cold-blooded betrayal—because they needed his specialisms? Was there something in him that never resigned himself to that traduction. What would he have become, if he'd stayed where he was? A cardinal? Was he genuinely scared of hell fire?'

'We mustn't be too controversial for peak-hour viewers,' Posnan said.

'No. But we've got to know the whole truth before we decide what to suppress. Pagendarm appears to have rejected Anna-Maria from the moment that Fromm made his *faux* pas. He wouldn't even see her in the nick. He avoided her when she paid his fine. He got on the coach. She got on with him. At the Postilion he gave the party the slip—perhaps by judicious use of the urinal. He went up the lane to the kennels. So did she—'

'You know all this for certain, do you?'

'No. I'm working it out. Tomorrow, I'll go over the ground.'

Posnan sat back and looked at him with a new expression.

'You know, Kenworthy, I followed one or two of your cases when you were a working copper. You had the reputation of being an arrogant sod. Was that when you were feeling least sure of yourself?'

'I don't know. There were times when I was so near to failure, I had to pre-empt myself. I had to make the sort of declaration that I couldn't turn back from.'

'And that always worked?'

'It often looked as if it had.'

'My God, Kenworthy—I'm going to enjoy this.'

A little while later, Posnan plugged in a video-player.

'Let's have a look at the programme so far. Sorry if that sounds like Morecambe and Wise.'

The familiar *Crucible* theme music: the *Danse macabre*, which the programme had brought within sight of the charts. Then followed a montage of highlights from previous editions: the tragic change in the face of the Royal Ulster Constable, too late as he recognized the trap: the entrepreneur of caravan-sites, making a pass with his hand.

Next, as the opening credits rolled, top moments in close-ups of the jury: the American evangelist with that look of sudden, comprehending concentration that he was apt to apply to the most commonplace situations; Pagendarm looking vacantly into space.

—This is the story of two men—

They were shown cartoon-fashion, first: a lieutenant-colonel in his Sam Browne; an SS Captain with his cap at a supercilious angle.

—Two men who are now known to their fellows in a somewhat different guise—

The Brigadier sweeping leaves; the lychgate, the hammer-beam roof, the offertory plate.

—The Brigadier has strong views on some subjects—

'They got in your way. You got your men on the line, sighted your covering fire. . . The next thing you knew, your axis of advance was choked by the peasantry. . . Of course they were a rabble—'

—A clip from archives: chaos on the road to Dunkirk; a still of a weeded widow, stiffly dead at a crossroads—

'So much for our protagonist. A good story needs an antagonist, too. In this case, also a figure not entirely unknown to *Crucible* viewers.'

—A reprise of the earlier graphic of the SS Captain—

Posnan was saving his thunder.

'There's a very rude word for men like you,' Kenworthy said.

'And I dare say you've been called the same thing to your face. Let's turn it on a bit—'

—Shot of Hedges, ironing the Brigadier's shirt—

'Coming, your bleeding lordship . . . Well, it happened this way, you see. The night before the attack, battle or no battle, it had to be guest-night over in the Elys' mess.

And yours truly, of course, had the job of driving his lordship over, and waiting half the bleeding night for him. And when we got back, there's the duty officer waiting with this so-called Dutch priest. And I had the job of making hot coffee for him. And I'd remember him anywhere. Those eyes; and that triangular line of whisker over his cheek—'

'That,' Kenworthy said, 'makes Hedges into a four-letter word too.'

'He came to me with this story, about the bet and so forth. I put it on ice. Everybody comes to me with stories. I'm a busier man than the Ombudsman. But we get a lot of duff stuff too, you can imagine. One of my researchers picked it up casually, fiddled around with it, got her teeth into it, went to St Baaf, saw the Burgomaster, got another recognition. And I thought, what a hell of a twist! And that was a story in itself—not one of the best, but a story—until Krause turned up.'

'It doesn't say much for Hedges.'

'He knows that himself now. He wishes he could undo every syllable of it. My reading is that he and the Brigadier had had a hell of a barney about something. Oh, I know it's hammer and tongs all their living day. But one had said something, the other had said something, and for once it all got too big for Hedges. He's in his young sixties. Devereux's in his eighties. He's left Hedges a legacy—at nineteen forty-five values. Hedges was looking ahead. He wrote to me, as do a thousand others a week. So now, Kenworthy, tell me how much time we have. And whatever you say, I shall halve.'

'Forty-eight hours,' Kenworthy said.

'One day for me, one for you. Yours ends at six tomorrow evening.'

'Thank God I'm not on your regular payroll.'

'No one knows where he might end up, Kenworthy.'

CHAPTER 17

The next morning Kenworthy moved: nothing of startling complexity: a phone-call to a taxi-driver of his own choice. And another to Anna-Maria: which was how she came to be driving with him round a confusion of right-angles until she was lost. Kenworthy then led her down a series of passages and yards that brought them into the blonde's excursion office from the rear. Thus into the street, and when she saw the standing coach, she knew what he was up to.

'Mr Kenworthy—you can't do this to me.'

'If I don't,' Kenworthy said, 'you're in for a thin time with Clingo and Mitchell.'

The morning bulletins had already announced that someone was helping with enquiries. Presumably Krause.

'Spare me this.'

'Get aboard and let's talk.'

'We can talk anywhere.'

'I also need to work over this place they call the Postilion.'

'You know too much, Mr Kenworthy. You always did.'

'But up to now never quite enough.'

So he took his seat beside her, and they were early arrivals aboard, with a good half-hour to wait.

'You should not have tried to conceal that you followed your husband on to the coach.'

'It was stupid of me. I was sweating on it that no one in that party of strangers would remember me. And I was right, wasn't I? Nobody has. But my mind was disturbed. I couldn't have borne it, Mr Kenworthy, to have been locked away while they bullied me.'

'You'll be lucky to escape that now. Tell me what happened.'

'I saw Hans Jürgen get on. He was running away from me. I had no idea why. I hung about for a few minutes, to give him time to feel more secure. I watched the seats fill up: Arabs, Dutch, Germans, one or two English.'

The same thing was happening now. A large Italian family were going to make a picnic of it, the fat mother unpacking salami and cheese.

'I paid the driver. It didn't worry him that I had no place booked. I flopped down beside Hans Jürgen. He shrank physically from me, turned his face away.'

'But he told you before long what it was about?'

'No, he didn't. From then till now I don't know.'

The coach was filling up. The driver came down the aisle counting heads.

'Would you like me to tell you?'

'I say it again, Mr Kenworthy—you know too much.'

'Does the name Hardtstrasse mean anything to you?'

'What has anything to do with the Hardtstrasse?'

'Did Hans Jürgen never know that you worked for the Hardtstrasse before you met him?'

They were moving forward in short lengths behind a Severnside sea-food van, sidling into the A40 lane at Shepherd's Bush. For a long time, Anna-Maria said nothing. Then she took her hand away from the side of her face.

'Somebody told Hans Jürgen that?'

'Somebody.'

'Where? When?'

'At the last *Crucible* session.'

'Who?'

Kenworthy was silent.

'All right,' she said. 'Maybe I don't need to be told. And maybe you never will forget your policeman's training.'

'It seems you've never forgotten yours.'

'Meaning the Hardtstrasse? Perhaps that wasn't quite what you thought it was. And it was a long time ago.'

'Long enough for your safety? I'm out of touch these days. I don't know what the current statute of limitations says. But you rank as one of my failures, Frau Pagendarm. If I'd known, in my Berlin days, what I could have put down to you—'

'Precious little, when the vapour had cleared. What's the penalty for priest-snatching? And he didn't come entirely unwillingly. After that—*pft*!'

She made a gesture as if that could have disposed of the issue. But Kenworthy gave no remission.

'Oh yes? Even during the war years? With a husband gaining high commendation in Minsk? We didn't have any women on trial in Nuremberg, did we? There were a few concentration camp guards, like Irme Grese at Belsen: but I'll grant you that they were a different kind of animal. Essentially it was a man's world. But you can't tell me that down the line there weren't a few peculiarly feminine chores being done.'

They were picking up speed now, already out in the 40 limit.

'If I told you the truth, you'd think it was feeble.'

'I'd take silence as weaker still.'

'You were always a fair man, Mr Kenworthy. More than one internment widow in Berlin told me that. Well: I was a good little Nazi girl—even before the Nazis took power. But you must judge that in the light of the propaganda we lived with. Is it terribly unnatural for a twelve-year-old to be a patriot? Or to embrace the action party, when the middle-class world is in ruins, alongside its values? I was a good little Nazi. I was senior patrol-leader in the Köln-Deutz branch of the *BdM*—the *Bund deutscher Mädchen*.'

'I do remember what that means.'

Blonde-braided, strapping young Aryans, the girls' Hitler Youth—open-air toughening courses, mountain camps with the pull of the old romantic songs.

'I trained as a secretary when I left school, but my *BdM* record wasn't lost on the big shots. You may say I was a fanatic. When I believe in a thing, I want to do something about it. I was recruited in the Hardtstrasse by a couple from the oldest days of the party: *goldenes Partei-abzeichen*—the gold award for those who'd stuck by the Führer since the days of the old beer-hall *Putsch*. I wasn't on the payroll. The job may seem mean to you: it was glamorous to me—listening for traitors, reporting subversive conversations. Do I defend myself too glibly? It was so: I was doing what I believed in. Then they recruited me officially to gain the services of this reputedly brainy young Catholic priest. As you know, I succeeded.'

Her English was grammatically, even colloquially superb, but there was an academic purity in her vowel sounds that would have stood in the way of her ever becoming a spy.

'I was meant to inveigle Hans Jürgen into the Clerical Directory post. I was not meant to fall in love with him and marry him. The standard biological trap? I loved Hans Jürgen for what he was—and because, too, I suppose, he needed my mothering. All of that—all the usual ingredients. And I was often bitterly sorry, too—for even a good little Nazi girl could have her sensitive moments, Mr Kenworthy. I was bitterly sorry when I saw his secret black suffering for what he saw as a sin, the negation of his vows. I have been a bad woman, Mr Kenworthy. I *am* a bad woman. So why shouldn't a bad woman marry a good man? I have done all the duty I could by Hans Jürgen: ever since I first tricked him.'

She fumbled in her bag for cigarettes, her fingers over-active, reinforcing her composure.

'I fell in love with him and married him without consulting the Hardtstrasse. That was the sort of impulsive young lady I was. There was consternation when they found out, but after the first pomposities, at least as far as the local office was concerned, they had a good laugh about it. I had no permanent position. I had completed my task. I had also given the job the best cover-story it could have had. I was an impeccable Nazi, now hog-tied to a man who was going to have to become an impeccable Nazi himself. What better combination? In higher quarters, they didn't think so. Gestapo girls of the calibre they wanted from me did not have affairs of the heart with the subjects of their assignments. So they dropped me. By the time we were fixed up in Berlin, and Hans Jürgen was really beginning to enjoy his card-index, we were low-average earners. That also helped the Berlin office to keep us where they wanted us: I couldn't afford to let Hans Jürgen fall down on his job.'

Kenworthy interrupted.

'You're not going to tell me that you stayed dropped—with feverish war preparations going on? And what contribution did you make to his SS commission?'

'Of course I didn't stay dropped. I was on again the moment they made me an offer. What do you think? And the SS commission—do you think I'd ever have gained anything by telling Hans Jürgen the truth about that? Oh, don't be so shocked, Mr Kenworthy. I can feel your puritanical distaste.'

'Not distaste,' he said.

'What, then—jealousy?'

A sudden sharp stab of provocation that came out involuntarily.

'Hardly, at this moment,' he said. 'I can see how you kept your two worlds apart. What I don't know is how you ever held them together.'

'Do you think such adventures ever mattered to me? Do

you think they made any difference to my feelings for
Hans Jürgen? If these things have to be done, they have to
be done. They don't take long. They're soon over and
done with.'

'It seems a strange sort of love to me.'

'*Love?* I don't know how you've done the job that you've
done all these years and learned so little about women.'

'My happier hours have been spent with women coping
with less sensational conflicts.'

'How do you know? Coping with similar conflicts in less
dramatic circumstances, perhaps. You blame me for
sleeping with an Obersturmbannführer in a vital
interest. There are plenty of women who sleep with their
husbands in the same spirit of pretence—and carry it off
with equal success.'

'But that's not how it was between you and Hans
Jürgen?'

'Certainly not.'

'That's what I fail to understand. I don't see him as the
dazzling light at the end of your weary day.'

'Because you know nothing of him. You remember only
the frightened, inarticulate wreck who'd just come out of
Haus Ehrlich: in suspense from minute to minute whether
you were going to send him westwards or eastwards.'

'I tried to bear that in mind at the time.'

'You didn't see, as I did, the moments of doubt, the
remorse for his sin. He believed in his God; I was
fortunate enough not to. I tried to assure him; I could
never convince him. There were terrible hours. Then
when he came out of Prisoner of War camp, he found a
new calm. It wasn't a new God he'd discovered, it was a
new attitude to his old one. But even that didn't go deep
enough. The old conscience kept breaking through: and I
always knew to the second when it had. At first, as a
Lutheran, he had an outlook as strict and as black-coated
as yours, Mr Kenworthy. I admit that it frightened me. I

did not know how I was going to live with it, in adventure-less peace-time. But then he went on a training course, about adapting his preaching to contemporary media. And he made a new discovery, by which I don't mean the technicalities. He discovered the manipulation of people's emotions. There were lectures on social psychology: nothing basically new to him, except that he started approaching people in a new, analytical way. He suddenly buckled down to it. It was what he needed. Throughout the time I knew him, the only time he was ever contented was when he was working flat out at some-thing. Whatever he did, he always did it as well as it could be done. Even Minsk. Now he was into mass responses. I used to laugh at him at first, the way he had everything docketed. He used to talk of *the weakness of emotional responses evoked by purely imaginary stimuli*. Then suddenly I saw that it was working. He was making it work, as determinedly and as efficiently as he had always made everything work. Hence the Radio Pastor. He was helped, of course, by his natural physical development. His features broadened, he let his hair grow—'

'And he was no longer disturbed by his memories?'

'Less so: but never quite free. He didn't believe in hell fire, Mr Kenworthy. At bottom he believed in something worse. I don't know what it was. Nor did he, in terms that can be talked about.'

They were overtaken by a yellow Capri, and a minute or so later they overtook the Capri: two drivers mitigating the boredom of the road.

'Did he have black memories too about the barbarities he had committed?'

'You know nothing about barbarities, Mr Kenworthy—you who have never been tempted, persuaded or blackmailed into them. It's only the first barbarity that counts, the first crushing of a man's jaw with a rifle-butt. More usually it's something less definite than that: the

stroke of an office pen that has an unknown man's jaw
broken by a rifle-butt in some location you've never even
heard of. When you've done it once, you can do it again.
Barbarity comes easily enough to man.'

'Or to woman. You haven't mentioned your own black
memories.'

'I have none. They would be a waste of my time.'

'You're a hard woman.'

'Which is why I still exist.'

'I find myself casually wondering how many you
engineered into gas-chambers, extermination camps.'

'Rather fewer than your RAF slaughtered in Hamburg
or Dresden.'

'We shall solve nothing by exchanging the arithmetic of
casualties. It's all over.'

'It isn't, Mr Kenworthy. It will go on for ever. It's only
the alignments that change. Next time, the expert on
partisans in the region of Minsk will be someone on your
side—you hope.'

They had arrived at the vast concrete Tudorism of the
Postilion.

'You aren't going to make me go in there?'

'You went in before?'

She answered with a facial shudder.

'Did he go with you?'

'No.'

The Italians were rising in their seats, assembling
children and lunch remnants without visible system.

'No. He went off alone, across the road.'

'You weren't tempted to go with him?'

'He said he wanted to be on his own. He wanted to
think things over. I saw hope in that. It was the first time
that morning that he showed signs of even thinking about
reconciliation.'

'You're sure he didn't go up there?'

Indicating the lane that led direct to the kennels:

Mitchell's men had done house-to-house up there, hadn't unearthed a thing. No one seemed even to see what their neighbours did, in this extra-suburban community.

'I told you, he crossed the road—went back along the way we had come.'

She said she couldn't face lunch. Kenworthy bought her a gin and tonic.

'In your trade, won't that count as an inducement?'

'I'm not in the trade any more. And it's the only inducement I can afford. So you stayed here in the pub until the coach moved on?'

'I never moved from that table over there.'

'So you were aware of the contretemps when the driver discovered he was two passengers short?'

'Contretemps? He seemed to think it was our fault.'

Kenworthy had become pensive. He did not rush into his next question.

'Doesn't it strike you as odd that there were *two* missing?'

The anomaly hit her.

'He said there were two missing. I suppose this is the moment at which you consider you've caught me out?'

'Not necessarily.'

'It strikes me now as extremely odd. I can't explain it. It didn't strike me as odd then. I was beyond thinking properly.'

'When you got back on the coach, why wasn't the whole thing explained by the fact that you were sitting alone?'

'People had changed seats all over the place. One of the Italian kids had taken mine. I sat somewhere else.'

'And you completed the coach tour?'

'Oh God, yes. I thought it was one way of filling in time. Hans Jürgen had had moods before. I expected him to come round in the end. My hope, indeed, my expectation, was that he would turn up at the hotel. When he didn't, I wasted my time reporting his disappearance at your famous Yard.'

At about a quarter to two, their driver started rallying the
party. Anna-Maria said she had better disappear for a
minute. Kenworthy also decided it was time for a
personal retreat. In his case it consisted of a fast silent
ascent of the staircase leading to the residents' bedrooms.
Here, when there was minor consternation below, when
the count showed somebody was missing, he was actually
in a broom-cupboard. With his ear to the thin panel of
the door, he listened to the flurry.

'History repeats itself.'

'Let's bloody hope not. The last bugger who got left off
Merrie England didn't do too well for himself.'

Kenworthy waited to hear the coach move off, then
found himself a back way out, crossed the road and
followed the direction Pagendarm was said to have taken.
He came to a nucleus of old village, bypassed by the dual
carriageway, its only frontage to the modern world a
small and rudimentary inn, the Anchor. He went into this
inn, whose trade looked essentially local, asking if there
was a phone he could use, and blustering a good deal.

'The self-centred sods! Just because I've slipped round
the back, they go off without me. And the buggers in the
road-house are not an atom of help. Every phone's either
in use or out of order. Do people often get left behind off
these coaches?'

'It's happened. Sometimes people like to get away from
the mob. Or perhaps they prefer a ploughman's and a
drop of real ale. Then of course they have to keep a
weather-eye open not to get left.'

'Did anyone come here that day—the day the German
was killed?'

The landlord was wary.

'If you're police, we've the right to be told so.'

'Not any more. Used to be. Name of Kenworthy.'

'Yes, well, there were two that day, but I can't think they'd be connected. And they went off in ample time not to get left.'

'What sort of people? A man and a woman?'

'Two men. Both old, one a lot older than the other. Military types. The older one spotted that Charlie here looked like an old soldier, and wanted to know what mob he'd been in.'

'They didn't want to know if anyone else from the coach had been in here?'

'Not a mention of it. The little chap did use the phone, but only to ring up his bookie.'

Kenworthy made his own phone-call. It was to arrange a time to be picked up by car.

'Not my business,' the landlord said, 'but if you want to save yourself wasted effort, there are no questions left to be asked here. The detectives who came asked them all. They learned nothing. If the German got up to Camerons' kennels, he got there unnoticed.'

'And could he have got there unnoticed?'

'He must have, mustn't he?'

'So how many ways are there from here to the kennels?'

'As many ways as a man's feet care to take him.'

'Meaning he didn't go in a straight line? He was walking at random? Across open fields?'

'Across open fields, behind hedges, through woodlands. If he wasn't breaking any laws or wearing a funny hat, there'd be no reason for anyone to pay any attention to him.'

Kenworthy left the pub, walked a few hundred yards back in the London direction, and when he was out of vision of the village, stopped and studied the Ordnance Survey map at some leisure. Then he walked on until he came to a Footpath Preservation Society's fingerpost establishing a right of way to a village two and a half miles distant. It led him between a hedge and a wire fence. It was in reasonably good trim and clearly in quite frequent use. It took one dog's leg turn to the right and another to the left. Near the second he met head-on with a woman with two toddlers crammed into a baby-buggy. He wished her good-afternoon and she barely responded, looking at him warily and moving on quickly. A minute or two later the path ceased to run between boundaries and branched into two at right angles along the edges of a pasture dotted with heaps of muck ready for spreading. He studied his map again, then, finding a fallen log, sat on it and put on his pipe.

Within the next ten minutes, three more people passed him: a middle-aged woman exercising a Scottie terrier; a hollow-backed gentleman with retired forces written all over him; and a man whom he had seen drinking in the Anchor. If this was average traffic along the path, Pagendarm must have been seen at least two or three times. And wouldn't there have been at least something in his bearing to make people remember him? Fear? Morbid introspection?

Mitchell's minions must have put direct questions, skilfully interpreting any hesitancy, to ninety per cent of the people in the village. What, then? It could have been a syndrome with which Kenworthy was over-familiar: the witness who suppressed his evidence, because he had private reasons for concealing that he had been on the scene: the scrim-shanking labourer, the poacher, the man whose wife thought him elsewhere. It was possible in one case, became a coincidence in two, was unacceptable in five or six. Chance, then? Chance was untidy, unscientific, led to untidy and unscientific conclusions. But chance existed.

The footpath came to a gap in the hedge, an open and broken gate, access for farm vehicles. Kenworthy went through it, the accumulation of a lifetime's acquired senses telling him that that was what Pagendarm would have done, if he had known that he was being followed. He passed a ditch-and-hedge hollow with crushed vegetation and a litter of cigarette-packets: a love-palette. Would Pagendarm have tried to go to ground there? Or would his military training have stood him in good stead? Would he have recognized a natural bolt-hole as a natural trap?

Kenworthy had almost passed the spot when he was halted by a rustle of foliage and an immature giggle. The hollow concealed a sort of dug-out, occupied by two boys, aged fourteen or fifteen, who were sniggering over a soft-porn magazine. Kenworthy had them out and petrified in seconds.

'Not supposed to be at school?'

He came eventually to the edge of a wood crossed by a trodden track: debris, a quantity of packaged food cartons. Pagendarm would have turned in here. Trees could be comforting, though these were too sparse to have given him much protection. But in a desperate man, a feeling of security was relative. And Pagendarm was desperate.

He had left no evidence of his passing. What evidence could he have left? He had not been engaged in a paper-chase, scattering clues to the hounds. Had Pagendarm known he was going to be killed? Even with his back to a wall, a condemned man clings to slivers of hope.

The path went through the wood along an irregular diagonal, came out into rough pasture where, as a visible path, it ceased to be. Kenworthy skirted a post-and-rail fence—hunted men do not like open spaces—and came to the shrubbery at the bottom of a prosperous villa garden, dense vegetation hiding all but the blue tiling of a small swimming-pool. Could a desperate man have broken in to hide in there? Not without breaking foliage; and none had been broken. Mitchell's men would not have missed a snapped twig.

Kenworthy continued, arriving at the perimeter fence of the boarding kennels: no baying of hounds, no whimpering of litters. Only a distant glimpse of barrack-like sheds and a corner of wire-meshed enclosure.

This, then, was where it had all ended? The curtain-scene opened by a declaration of revenge? Pagendarm had been facing his attacker: that was evident from powder-burns. How long had he stood looking into the automatic? He had had his right shoulder towards the kennel-grounds at the moment of falling: Mitchell had determined that from the lie of the corpse. Kenworthy turned and faced the same way himself: learned nothing by it.

They had heard no shot, then, in the kennels or the house? Probably not. Apparently not. No disturbance among the dogs? None reported. It had passed, then, as something not out of the ordinary: the same sort of momentary unrest that might have been aroused by a passing cat?

Kenworthy retraced his footsteps, quickly now, because he did not want to keep his transport waiting. Posnan was coming for him himself.

'Sorry,' Kenworthy said. 'Will one blunderbuss apology do? There'll be no solution by six o'clock today.'

'Never mind. We're not through yet. Can you imagine how many of our ideas get no further than the script-typist? Tell me what you do know.'

'Mostly what I don't.'

Kenworthy summarized. Posnan did not need to ask supplementaries.

'The evidence of the truants is worthless. They saw a man. They saw another man. They saw a woman. Their descriptions are valueless.'

'Utterly,' Kenworthy said. 'But we could use them—'

'Only as a last resort. Let's eliminate. Let's hope it

wasn't the Brigadier. That would be too neat and trivial—even for one of my shows. But I can hear his reasoning, can't you, "There's the chap who was responsible for what they tried to blame me for. Comes to this country with his pocket full of German marks and starts lifting stuff from our shops. Time someone taught the bugger a lesson." '

'No,' Kenworthy said.

'No. Let's try Hedges, then. Dead scared about what's going to happen to him when the Brigadier finds out about his betrayal. But no one speaks ill of the dead, so do away with Pagendarm and there won't be a programme.'

'No.'

'Pity—but no. Where do you go next, Kenworthy?'

'Start from this thought: how did Devereux and Hedges come to be on the coach? Because they'd seen Pagendarm get on. Because, therefore, they'd been in court. Which means that they must have seen a brief item in the *Evening Standard*, probably in the Stop Press, next door to the late racing results. So how many other people saw that item?'

'God knows how many, the life he's led.'

'We've ruled out Krause, we've ruled out Fromm. Let them stay ruled out, for the sake of progress. Why does it have to be someone we already know about? This isn't a book we're writing, where nothing must come up in the last chapter that hasn't been neatly provided for.'

'Kenworthy, I can't say you play blind man's buff particularly well, but you do play it elegantly.'

'Meaning what?'

'Meaning you haven't mentioned Anna-Maria.'

He pulled them off the road into a lay-by. The driver of a TIR articulated was urinating into a ditch.

'Look at it, Kenworthy: we have only Anna-Maria's word for it that she stayed on the coach. How many dozen

reasons can you think of why Pagendarm should suddenly
have turned on her? She follows him to argue with him.
It's not her gun he's running away from, it's her tongue.
It's only in final exasperation that her gun comes out.
She's just the woman to have such a fire-arm, isn't
she?'

'I hope not.'

'Why do you hope not? For the reputation of your
judgement?'

'No. The only judgement that matters to me is my final
judgement, and I haven't made that yet about Anna-
Maria. Will the expense-sheet run to a trip to Spain?'

'What the hell do you want to go to Spain for?'

'To talk to a coach-driver on holiday.'

'He'll remember nothing.'

'He might if he's helped.'

'Don't be out of London more than twelve hours, then.
Home Counties TV have been standing by all day with
captions and graphics at the ready, waiting to announce a
sensational change of evening programme.'

CHAPTER 18

'Bloody bad show,' the Brigadier said. 'Must be in my
dotage, not co-operating with law and order. Ought to be
shot at dawn. Probably will be, eh?'

He laughed with unexpectedly falsetto overtones, a
touch of hysteria. In the other room, Hedges was
knocking about, obviously straining his ears.

'Had to make a decision somewhere along the line.
Settled for not being involved. Might have been misunderstood, you know. Took a chance, and obviously you
were too clever for me. Ought to have expected it.'

A figure on the edges of farce, foolish and honourable.

Paternalistic, traditionalist, simplistic—and not far from senile.

'Saw that bit in the paper. Felt damned sorry for the poor devil. Shop-lifted myself once, you know, saw exactly how it must have come about in his case. Pinched a comb from Woolworth's counter once, in the old days, before they started locking you in behind check-outs. Not because I intended to rook them. I'd stood about so long, trying to catch a young lady's eye to come and serve me. The old patience ran out. But at least I had the decency to send them ninepence anonymously through the post.'

Kenworthy's short evening was very full. But he did not hurry the Brigadier.

'So I said to Hedges, "Well, we'll go and sit in the back of the court." Had a sort of fellow-feeling for the chap, you know. Cut-throats against each other one minute, the next you're old friends. You've been through something together, you see. Been through the very same thing, when all's told. I could have wept for the poor devil in the dock. Distant—too ashamed to raise his eyes. When it was over, all he wanted to do was get clear of the court, away from anyone who knew him. I said to Hedges, "Let's go after him and buy him a pint. Let him see he's not entirely without friends." Saw him get on the coach, so we got on too.'

There was still a remnant of unspent eagerness in the Brigadier's eyes.

'Besides, there was something else I wanted to say to him. Wanted to let him know there was no bitterness because of what had transpired through *Crucible*. He was using those refugees, you know, to work saboteurs through our lines. But that night that he came to see me at my forward HQ, I couldn't tell him there was going to be an attack in the morning. Had to keep him in the dark about it. But all he had to do with his refugees was sit tight. The next day, they'd all have been inside our line,

anyway. So after a fashion, he wasn't at fault for beating
his flock on to our guns.'

The old man was talking himself breathless.

'Anyway, I never got the chance. When he got off the
coach, we saw him cross the road, running away even
from the woman now. So I said to myself, There's a man
who prefers his own company. Not the best time for
swapping war yarns with him: man's got other things on
his mind. And then we saw this other pub across the road,
and I said to Hedges, "What-ho for a hunk of bread and
cheddar and a pint of clean wallop?" '

'But you did get back to the Postilion in time for the
coach?'

'Oh God, yes. Couldn't have afforded to have missed it.
Would have cost a month's spirit ration to have got
ourselves back from that blasted spot.'

'Did you notice whether the woman, Frau Pagendarm,
was still with the party?'

'Couldn't tell you, old man, people hadn't stuck to
their own seats. Swanning about all over the place.
Foreigners, a lot of them.'

Kenworthy left him and made a final, more or less
hopeless attempt through some of his fringe-world
contacts in secret places to contact a man called Piper,
who had once been a Captain with one of the MI's.

CHAPTER 19

Fletcher woke with a tongue like a sour face-flannel in his
hotel in Torremolinos. It was a large hotel, 2,000 guests,
almost all British, with its own swimming pool (for some
technical reason empty throughout the Fletchers' visit)
and Bingo from eight every evening till four every
morning. Near at hand was a *Taberna*, run by two

brothers from Ashton-under-Lyne, who sold fish and chips and Watney's ales.

Fletcher did not take kindly to being wakened by the house-phone before eight in the morning when he had been barely three hours in bed. It was even less joy to him that the man waiting for him in the manager's office was self-evidently a London policeman. Fletcher had seen enough of life to recognize the brand. He was not subtle enough to spot signs of retirement (if there were any). Kenworthy took no steps to dispel his misconceptions.

Fletcher was even less pleased to learn that this bogey had flown overnight to ask questions about passengers missing from that last Merrie England trip. The incident had not come into his mind again since the afternoon of the excursion. He had not even thought of reporting it at the garage; that might have meant hanging about. Who gave a bugger for the sort of shower that went on those bloody outings? Moreover, he had not seen a London paper since leaving home.

But he was wary of this London rozzer. For one thing, Kenworthy was unmitigatedly nasty with him from the moment of their meeting. Anyone would have thought that Kenworthy suspected him of some crime. Within very few minutes, it was explicit that Kenworthy did think he had committed a crime: but he was in no hurry to say what. Fletcher began to sweat. He knew, or thought he knew, that it didn't matter all that much whether you'd committed a crime or not, if the Old Bill had decided to hang it on to you.

'What's so important about some bloody steamer who can't be bothered to be back on time?'

'It starts to matter the moment the poor bloody steamer snuffs it.'

'Yes, well, OK, if that's the case, I'm sorry. But it's not down on my slate. I don't even know who it was who *was* missing.'

'No? We've picked up sign that says otherwise. We know it was set up—and no simple set-up at that. It included taking bloody good care that you did set off without him.'

'Hey, Christ, don't try that on, brother. We left quarter of an hour overdue, and that's fatal on these bloody capers. It piles up, one stop after another, and then you're into a late meal and waiters' overtime.'

'All right, Fletcher, spare me the economics. Do you want to be straight about things now, or do you want a scheduled flight back from Malaga airport in an hour and a half's time?'

'Don't make me laugh. You've extradition and all that to consider.'

'True. And if you want a spell in a Spanish nick while the lawyers sort it out, you are welcome.'

'What do you want to know?'

'How many people were missing when you drove off from the Postilion?'

'Two. There's no argument about that.'

'Two what? Two men? Two women?'

'I don't know. I only look at their tickets.'

'Except when they get on without tickets. Then you only look at their cash. We'll have that on the consideration sheet, shall we?'

Fletcher closed his eyes in nausea.

'Ask anything you like,' he said. 'I'll tell you anything you want to know. But what I don't know, you'll have to bloody well whistle for.'

'Two people,' Kenworthy said. 'Think hard.'

'It's no use bloody thinking.'

'Two old men, perhaps? One older than the other?'

But Fletcher did not hear that. He had remembered something else.

'Of course, if you look at it another way, there were three missing.'

'What way of looking at it is that, then?'

'I wasn't counting the German.'

'Why not?'

'You see, he'd got on the coach like a man with something on his mind: like as if he was catching the last bus by the skin of his teeth. And I said to him, "Save your breath for the final sprint, mate. We don't leave for another twenty minutes." But he wouldn't calm down. Couldn't even get his money right. And I had to practically push the change into his hand.'

'Lost a chance there, didn't you?'

'I may have a bit of a fiddle on the side, but I stick to a fair price.'

'Well, was the German one of those who were missing? You paid enough attention to him when he got on. Surely you remember—'

'That's what I'm coming to. When he got off at the Postilion, he sort of kept his distance from the others. And he came up to me as I was locking the coach and said, "I'm calling on someone I know in this village. If I'm not back in time, don't hold the party up for me." That's why I didn't count him in the check-up. And, that way of looking at it, there were three missing.'

'Which way did he go? Did he cross the road?'

'I don't know. I didn't look.'

'Did anyone go after him?'

'I couldn't say. I get two free pints at the Postilion for a party that size. I went in to claim them.'

Kenworthy took him over it again, played the usual tricks to try to tempt him to change major points or add something forgotten. But the pattern now remained firm.

'By the way, Fletcher, I wouldn't like to face any aggro for attempting to impersonate a Metropolitan policeman. Any such misunderstanding has been a case of auto-suggestion on your part. Understand?'

'What the hell do you mean? Who are you, Kenworthy?'

'Let's say, an interested party.'

Kenworthy left. Fletcher went back to his room and an Alka-Seltzer. The *Taberna* with the canned English beer wouldn't be open for nearly four hours yet.

CHAPTER 20

When Kenworthy arrived home, Elspeth gave him a message the moment he set foot in the house. Would he telephone a man called Piper? And Piper, when he rang, said that it had come to him along a grapevine that Kenworthy had been trying to contact him. An hour and a half later, the contact was made.

Piper had changed from the young captain in Berlin, who had been a contrast to the orthodox major. Four or five years older than Kenworthy, he had aged in a different way—towards a constant conservation of effort in all things. But something barely definable remained about him: the natural courtesy of a man who as a three-pipper had treated a three-striper with respect. He, too, had retired—he did not say from what—and he said that he had guessed at once, since their paths had crossed for an aggregate of only about twenty minutes, that it could only be about one subject.

'And what bloody amateurs we were at it, Kenworthy. Most of our American oppos had at least been federal dicks.'

'We got some things done,' Kenworthy said.

'And how much wool was being pulled over our eyes? What's the trouble, anyway?'

'Operation Schultze.'

'Yes—it had to be that. He survived, did he? I had an

inkling he would: with a wife like that, and full fees to Peter Fromm. But I lost touch, you know. I was demobilized less than two months after you were.'

'All I need to know is what infiltrators you had with that group *über die grüne Grenze*.'

'None,' Piper said, and paused to let it sink in. 'Oh hell, no. When I put up the scheme to my bosses, there was all hell up. Contriving the escape of a man who was on the Moscow Wanted List, as agreed by the Big Four at Yalta? Wasn't it time I toddled round to be seen by the psychiatrist? No; it didn't matter two hoots what gen we'd get out of it. And no matter what nefarious arrangements I'd already started, we left it strictly alone. We forgot it.'

Kenworthy rubbed out dark flake and filled his pipe.

'And, of course, somebody started remembering what had gone on in Minsk. Schultze had done what might be called a thorough job: a couple of hundred machine-gunned here and there to make sure of getting the one he wanted.'

'But not Schultze's finger on the trigger?'

'Are you still trying to defend him, Kenworthy?'

'Far from it. He set it all up—but he'd steer clear of the death-sites. He called the tune—but I never thought he'd the guts to play the fiddle.'

Piper's face said that he agreed, but that none of it mattered.

'And you were lucky, you know, Kenworthy. When I picked up your note in the Berlin office that you'd set the ball rolling, there was talk of bringing you back off demobilization leave to face charges: exceeding your duty.'

And Kenworthy, cold, the adrenalin bristling his spine, pictured what that could have done to his life: being taken away from Elspeth again after the parted years; the court-martial—he'd not have got off that one with a severe rep; the backlash on his promotion in the Met.

They could have asked him to resign.

Piper saw that he was disturbed, but misread the reason for it.

'Oh, don't think I blamed you. You had to make a decision. You made it in the interests of the job as you saw it. But you know how it was with some of the dug-outs: the thing wasn't rounded off if a head hadn't rolled.'

And the whisper had been that he'd lost his head over a woman? But Piper didn't say that, didn't even hint at it. Didn't even think it—?

'In the end, sense prevailed. Why blow it up? Let it die. Schultze just hadn't happened. He hadn't been through our hands. And as, in fact, he'd only been through yours, there was only one file to destroy.'

'And no man who was travelling with that group was a plant?'

'Not of ours.'

'A Russian plant, then?'

'Who can say? We'd assumed they'd let Schultze escape. It would also be logical to assume that they'd follow him up. But who talks of logic where the NKVD are concerned? They were inscrutable. They were also capable—what intelligence service isn't?—of monumental clangers.'

'I know: but this pair I'm interested in—they didn't even finish the course.'

'That would figure. Where and when did they drop out?'

'A day or two short of the last lap: pushing up towards Lübeck and the Baltic.'

'That would fit in. By then they'd have mapped out the whole escape-route: the collaborating farmers, bargees, weaknesses in patrols and control-posts. Maybe some of Fromm's most precious peasants disappeared overnight. We would never know. Who would ever know? What were their names, by the way?'

'Tradern and Lerche.'

'No. They ring no bells. But what's a name? We shall never know, Kenworthy. Some farm-labourer might have done them in for any wealth they were carrying—or were thought to be carrying. They may have been flushed out of some hole by a local patrol, and simply been cut off from Fromm's party. And nerves got wracked, you know, on these desperate journeys. There were tales of men murdered by their fellow travellers.'

Piper called for whisky.

'In five years of war, Kenworthy, twelve million disappeared into the grey landscape. And in the year after it, there were hundreds of thousands on the move: some trying to get home, some trying to put as much distance between them and home as they could. Others were happy just as long as they were still moving. It was unhealthy to ask a stranger a question. And in what passed for a green belt round Berlin, if a man said his name was this or that, nobody cared whether he was to be believed or not.'

And Kenworthy remembered a moment of salutary lavatory humour, at dawn on a frontier railway station: two thousand men, some on leave, some discharged: artisans, civil servants, teachers, wages clerks, family men, all in the facelessness of earth-coloured battledress, but all going one way, and all for once knowing why. And one frosted window was run up on the plea from the Tannoy to hold on to his excrement.

'Bugger your bloody luck, chum.'

CHAPTER 21

Activity was furious. Posnan had three production teams working with the frenzy of newsmen meeting a late afternoon deadline. One was concerned with a small group of extras, deployed with superb camera skill to look like a crowd, making a Merrie England tour of their own round a circuit of Chiltern villages. The second was out in a belt of pines on the sandy edge of the Norfolk Breckland—because there was no reason why the viewing public should not mistake a belt of pines in the Norfolk Breckland for a so-called green belt in the bleak anonymity of Central Europe. The third was riffling with practised speed through the indexes of archives.

There had been top-level conferences at Home Counties TV. The law had been laid on the line even for such an idol as Posnan. If Clingo's army moved to an arrest before the programme was screened, then the programme was off. And *Crucible* would not be naming the final personality. *Crucible* only asked questions; they had to be so simple and direct that even Clingo would have to act on the answers. But the nature of the ultimate innuendo had to be irretrievably scrambled, in case of an acquittal in the courts.

'That won't happen,' Kenworthy said.

'Pre-empting yourself again?' Posnan asked him.

'She's not going to defeat me this time.'

'If you get that woman on this programme, I shall believe you capable of anything.'

'We'll wait and see, shall we?'

The penultimate interview with Anna-Maria took place in her hotel room, over afternoon tea-things wheeled in on a trolley with a touch of Edwardian trimmings.

'This is something you simply can't do to me, Mr Kenworthy. You can't and you wouldn't.'

'I would, I can and I am going to,' Kenworthy said, his manner as agreeable as that of a bank manager offering an interest-free bridging loan.

'I'll not do it. I'll go back to Germany. I'll put myself under the protection of those nice men at Scotland Yard. I'll get on to the press about harassment.'

'You'll do none of these things when you've heard what I'm going to say.'

'Mr Kenworthy—how can you expect it of me? My husband had been on the jury-panel of *Crucible* since its inception. You'd expect me to sit under those lights and those cameras—and not break my heart?'

'Is it breakable, Frau Pagendarm? Or is it a transplant already forty years old?'

'Mr Kenworthy!'

'Frau Pagendarm—I stretched a point for you at the end of the war. Less and less, in the passage of the last two weeks, have I understood why I did that. I am stretching a point for you now, if only you will be patient enough to listen to me.'

She went through the motions of taking burlesque command of herself; but then relapsed into acid comment.'

'You're stretching a point for Max Posnan, you mean.'

'Frau Pagendarm, before this calendar year is out, you are going to be sentenced in an English Crown Court to imprisonment for life. That means, as things go at present, approximately fourteen years, which with average remission will bring it down to about ten. You will be a little over seventy when you come out.'

'And for what am I going to go to prison for life?'

'For the murder of Hans Jürgen Pagendarm, erstwhile Helmut Schultze, on the Buckinghamshire-Hertfordshire border, at about a quarter past three on Thursday—'

'Oh no! That is a charge that could never be brought. I may have been stupid. I may have panicked and told idiotic lies about my movements. But the murder—'

'Is down to you. And the charge is going to stick.'

'Not without a good deal of fabricated evidence.'

'Which is lying in the basket ready—all beautifully co-ordinated.'

For the first time, she was wondering whether to believe him. There was doubt in her eyes, and beyond doubt the beginnings of fear. She dismissed it by visible effort.

'Co-ordinated by you, Mr Kenworthy? You deeply disappoint me.'

'I would have thought that to one of your background, this sort of procedure would seem normal.'

'Meaning what? Meaning something I haven't touched for four decades? You're making too much of these so-called Gestapo connections of mine, Mr Kenworthy. I told you, after my marriage, they dropped me. I never was established. If it hadn't been for what Hans Jürgen was worth to them, I'd have been even further out in the cold. When the war broke out, and things deteriorated, I was called in sometimes on the fringes—to help out in situations where no patriot could have refused. It amounted to no more than producing evidence against subversives.'

'Subversives? In a world where a man could go to his death for criticizing the government over his Saturday-night pot? Very moving. An English court will appreciate that as character evidence: your experiences on the Gestapo fringes. They will be touched to see you make light of it. But as far as the mentality of our policemen is concerned, you made a crucial and unforgivable mistake: you told downright and unnecessary lies about whether you were on that coach. It was unlike you, Frau Pagendarm, to be so thrown off balance that you did not think things out properly. Perhaps you thought you were safe from that milling, impersonal, polyglot bunch, each little group so wrapped up in itself that no one was paying attention to outsiders. But alas, you have been remembered: by two passengers and the driver.'

'So? That proves that I told a silly lie—which in any case I admit. Do they not therefore give me an alibi? You are not going to say that two passengers and the driver saw the murder?'

Kenworthy ignored the point.

'Other people have remembered things, too. Two boys playing hookey from school—do you know our English phrase *hookey*, Frau Pagendarm? They did not come forward in the first round of questioning because they had no right to be where they were. But there's been an amnesty on their truancy now, and their statements are on the file. A man driving a tractor—you did not think he had seen you—saw a man enter a wood, and a woman not far behind him, not many minutes before a shot was fired. There was a man raking garden rubbish behind a shrubbery: did you really think that our Hertfordshire countryside was as unpopulated as it looked?'

'Mr Kenworthy—this is entirely fabricated.'

'And what if it is?'

Kenworthy looked at her pitifully. This was opening up a distinctly new possibility to her.

'I said, what if it is, Frau Pagendarm?'

'I cannot believe that English gentlemen—'

'You would be safer to look on the English gentleman as a mere product of Goebbels' propaganda. You are not dealing, Frau Pagendarm, with the kid-gloved detectives of vicarage tea-party fiction. You are dealing with men who have a case to break—and that under pressure. They are not dishonest men—at bottom. They have no doubt who the killer was, so they see nothing immoral in making sure that they have a case that will stand up.'

'Thank you for telling me. I am sure that my advocate will make sawdust of the evidence. And I shall see that you are sub-poenaed yourself.'

Kenworthy laughed.

'I flatter myself that any court in the land will treat me as a credible witness.'

'If any of what you are saying is in any respect true, Mr Kenworthy, why haven't they arrested me?'

'They are negotiating in the Federal Republic to get an affidavit from another key witness.'

'And who is that, may I ask?'

'Peter Fromm.'

It might have been a body blow; but she simply took time to digest it.

'Peter Fromm will know nothing.'

'There comes an end to knowing nothing, Frau Pagendarm: as you are about to find out. You have progressively told me more and more truth as the years have gone by. When you first walked into my life at the Charlottenburg fair, you weren't even expecting to have to admit Schultze of Minsk. One way or another, we have gradually expanded the story together, you and I. You have gone on suppressing what you thought could still be safely suppressed. But this is the ultimate.'

She looked at him steadily.

'And you are about to offer me a way out?' she said at last.

'You don't believe me, do you?'

She thought for a full half-minute.

'You want me to make a startling revelation on *Crucible*, is that it?'

'I want you to tell the truth on *Crucible*.'

'Why don't I simply tell the truth to Superintendent Mitchell and Commander Clingo?'

'Because you might find it very hard work getting them to believe you. And will they act on it, even if they do?

Whereas if you tell the truth to our great viewing public, and it is banner headlines in their morning papers, won't even Clingo's and Mitchell's hands be forced? In any case, what's your reason for fighting shy of the truth? Merely sentimental?'

'I am a very sentimental person, Mr Kenworthy.'

'So I have noticed.'

'As far as one man is concerned, I have been wholly consistent.'

'It's the only thing I hold in your favour,' he said.

Her eyes filmed over, but she did not cry.

'Use your brains, Frau Pagendarm. What danger is the truth to you? You are ruined anyway, at no matter what level you scramble out of this. Hans Jürgen's image is broken. Your home is as good as destroyed. You have lost all your friendships. But if I know anything of you, you'll find your way out of the rubble.'

'Not this time,' she said. 'Not again.'

'That may be be how you feel at this moment. I think you will prefer that kind of ruin to gaol.'

And she suddenly made herself brighten.

'What guarantee are you offering me?'

'None. You ought to know better than to ask. Everything is going to depend on the degree of conviction you can put over.'

'It will be horrible.'

'You won't enjoy it. But I'll spare you all I can.'

'*You*?'

'I shall be asking the questions on *Crucible*. There won't be many, and the session will be recorded in private.'

'Under those lights! I ask you to believe me, Mr Kenworthy: you were never in a position to appreciate Hans Jürgen. You can never have been. You only knew him when he was at the bottom of his misery. And Haus Ehrlich had left him barely in control of his mind. I

remember those days in Cologne when, although he
started off as my assignment, I was also discovering him. I
think of our times together on wartime leave in Paris. I
think of those days before your bombing got really bad,
and there was still gaiety in Berlin, wonderful radio
dance-music in our flat—'

In the days when Kenworthy had been courting
Elspeth . . .

'Even in those rock-bottom months when our income
had stopped, when I was making heavy weather of my
miscarriage, and he was failing at door-to-door
selling—we were an entity. We presented our own screen
to the world. Of course you didn't know him. Anything
you did for us, you did for me, didn't you?'

Kenworthy did not answer.

'Isn't that true, Mr Kenworthy?'

Her resilience was remarkable.

'Don't be a sulky bear, Mr Kenworthy. I have met your
wife. I know that in your life there have been no loop-
lines. Do you remember your moral homilies in my flat?
You must admit that getting us out of Berlin was *my*
work.'

'Why are you so anxious that I should admit that?'

'Because it's all over now, Mr Kenworthy, and the great
thing is to know that one did what one could.'

The great thing was that she had taken his bait. He
accompanied her from the hotel to the studio. There was
no question of letting her out of his sight at this stage.
There were still chances for things to go wrong: everything.

CHAPTER 22

Danse macabre—the background music and the opening credits—the highlight montage from Crucibles *of fame—the Ulster Defence Man—the internal stresses of Vietnamese Boat People, 'settled' on a housing estate in a north-western cotton town— shots of Fromm's travellers at moments of dawning truth—*

'This is the story of two men. Or, at least, it set out as the story of two men. It has ended up as the story of a man and a woman.'

Graphics—the Brigadier, with an unfair exaggeration of blimpishness—Schultze-Pagendarm, featureless Nazi—

'The story we had originally intended to tell was the clash of two purposes, in the war-weary Holland of 1944.'

Archive stills—muddy fields motionless in the suspended animation of autumn.

'This is where SS Hauptsturmführer Helmut Schultze, in the guise of a Dutch priest, threw thirty defenceless refugees into the teeth of a British battalion in action, all for the sake of planting three intruders behind the front line. Brigadier John Devereux, then a lieutenant-colonel commanding the vanguard, has this to say—'

A new recording of Devereux, the session with the Dutchmen scrapped—no sweeping up leaves—no offertory plate—

'I thought he was the village priest. He came to see me overnight and I told him to wait. Fortunes of war, you know. Couldn't very well have told him we were going to attack. If he'd only waited, he needn't have crossed our line at all. Our line would have crossed him.'

A confident Brigadier, utterly satisfied now it had

boiled down to this—no mention at all of Hedges—
'About Helmut Schultze, the *Crucible* team has elicited some interesting facts.'
Cologne: pre-war photographs—the priest and the lady, studio-acted, silhouettes without features—the sad flat in the Ruhr, their savings gone—Berlin, 1936, '37—a man's back, bent over ribboned documents— sinister men in felt hats—the midnight arrest of a priest—
'War. And SS Sturmführer Schultze serves in France in the relative peace that follows the capitulation. Then comes war on the eastern front. Schultze's specialized knowledge finds a fresh outlet—'
Archive and studio film indistinguishably mixed—a mass hanging in an unspecified grey urban square—
'Small wonder that at the end of hostilities Schultze was a candidate for interrogation by the NKVD—now more notorious as the KGB of our times. He was taken to an infamous country mansion in what is now called the Democratic Republic of East Germany.'
Shot of God knows what country property, lost behind barbed wire and pines—patrol dogs—Red Army guards—a civilian being struck across the jaw by a thickset man of Mongolian feature—
'For a man of Schultze's antecedents there was no more dangerous city in Europe than Berlin. Yet here again our hero—if we have settled on the right word—made good his escape. He was driven back into the ruined city in a lorry loaded with frost-bitten vegetables.'
Shot of the lorry (in the Norfolk Breckland: it appeared to be carrying sugarbeet)—the wreck of Berlin's Gedächtniskirche—*no reference to his passage through British hands—*
'Thanks to an organization that we shall not name, for fear of compromising others who found their way to a new life, Herr Schultze once again took to the wild

country, reinforced by a new identity. There were many things that money could buy in those years immediately after the holocaust.'

A meal at midnight in a cabaret beside a suburban lake—refugees on the move at night (through the Norfolk pines)—a road-block—a rubber stamp across the corner of a passport photograph—figures crawling through undergrowth on the blind side of an otherwise occupied sentry—

'Shall we ever know the true names of those who made up that party? For two or three weeks they made their way, largely at night, across the treacherous winter plains. We have labels for some of them: Herr and Frau Schultze, and two itinerants known to the others as Lerche and Tradern.

'Lerche was a little man, not without a sense of humour, a man with the sardonic outlook of a soldier who has survived what no soldier has the right to expect to survive. The other, Tradern, was a more sanguine, less talkative character: a man who had also survived, but whose survival had left him with thoughts that he preferred to keep to himself.

'A striking feature of these men was the close friendship between them. But they were regarded as something of an enigma by their companions. Could they have been moles, planted in the group by the NKVD, for the sake of exposing the escape-route? Or even by our own intelligence service, for precisely the same purpose? Throughout the journey, Lerche and Tradern were treated with wholesome suspicion by the other pilgrims.

'Then, one night when the party was dispersed among several neighbouring farmsteads, shots were heard in the vicinity—'

A timber-framed North German farmhouse in a cleft of rising valley lined by nocturnal pines—a blurred figure crawling into an ambushing position overlooking

the farm group—close-up of the farmhouse door, two
men, a yard or two apart, on an errand to a wood-
shed—the raider raising and steadying a heavy hand-
gun—two shots—one man, the one nearer the door,
falls crumpled—the other runs for cover, away from
the buildings—a third shot obviously wings him—
'Who fired those shots? It has never been established.
Suffice it to say that neither Lerche nor Tradern rejoined
the party the next morning to continue the trek across the
Communist-occupied belt.

'But one of those who did reach the safety of the British
zone was Schultze—having now taken the name of Pagendarm, the identity that he had bought through that
organization that we shall not name. Posing as an ex-
battery surveyor, a corporal in field artillery, he was now
able to transfer himself, through normal prisoner of war
channels, to his ultimate discharge and rehabilitation.
And it seems that the former SS Hauptsturmführer still
had leanings to one kind of priesthood or another. And of
his undoubted success in that role, there is no need for us
to assure our viewers. In his homeland, his prestige was
even greater—'

The Radio Pastor, at work in his Westphalian home—
stills from a magazine article, prosperity and comfort—
reprises of his more pensive moments in the Crucible
jury-box—
'And so to events of a recent October Thursday in our
own Home Counties, when Pagendarm shocked his wide
European congregation by his conviction before London
magistrates on a shop-lifting charge. We do not know the
reasons for this strange lapse of conduct, but it has been
suggested that he wanted to place himself under the
strongest protection that the capital can offer, because he
knew that he had at last been tracked down by someone
from his complex past. This suspicion gains added
strength when we consider the rapidity with which, at the

end of his hearing, he sought refuge in a standing tourist coach.'

Appropriate highlights from a reconstructed Merrie England tour—

'On the first scheduled halt of that tour, three people disappeared. They were Pagendarm, his wife—and a third character. Frau Pagendarm tells us that at the sight of this man, she abandoned all attempt to intervene. She knew that he could not pursue two at once, so she went off in a different direction from her husband, eventually getting herself back to London by long-distance coach.'

Sequence from the rear of a man stumbling uphill along a field footpath, pursued by another who was gaining on him at a rapid walk—schoolboys in a hedge-bottom—disappearance of first man round corner of hedge—second man follows, still narrowing gap— echoing shot disturbs birds—

'It is not for *Crucible* to attempt to furnish a solution. It is for viewers to make up their own minds. In order to help them in their decision, instead of our usual jury verdict, we present tonight a brief interview between Frau Pagendarm and Mr Simon Kenworthy, the distinguished retired Chief Superintendent from New Scotland Yard. For the sake of Frau Pagendarm's feelings, this interview will be brief.'

Throughout, the camera looked down at Frau Pagendarm over Kenworthy's shoulder—

KENWORTHY: We are old friends, Frau Pagendarm.

FRAU PAGENDARM: Yes, we have known each other a long time—since Berlin in the aftermath of war.

KENWORTHY: If there is one thing I have always admired about you, Frau Pagendarm, it has been your devotion to your husband. You have stood by him in more than one desperate position.

FRAU PAGENDARM: It moves me greatly to hear you say that, Mr Kenworthy. I do not think that I could have done more.

KENWORTHY: But at the sight of one man, a newcomer to the Merrie England coach, you let him go in one direction while you turned in another. Why was that?

FRAU PAGENDARM: Because I knew that this encounter was going to be terminal, and that there was nothing I could do about it. I knew this man, and I could not mistake the fanaticism in his eyes. He meant death, and the death of two of us could not have undone the death of one.

KENWORTHY: Was there no time to call for police protection?

Frau Pagendarm did not answer, and made it clear by the immobility of her features that she preferred not to do so.

KENWORTHY: Where had you seen this man before?

FRAU PAGENDARM: He had been our companion *über die grüne Grenze*. He was one of a pair about whom none of us had felt comfortable. I did discover— because men can give away a lot in their conversation with a woman— that he and his comrade had been soldiers together in the East. There was a deep friendship between them. They had come through a lot of misery together. Then one night they disappeared, which seemed to confirm our opinion that they were undercover agents. But I know what happened, though I do not know the subsequent history of Lerche. He was hurt that night, and I think he may have had to go to ground in Eastern Germany. That happened to others, and some of them were lucky. I do not know how, or when, he ever managed to get himself out again. I doubt whether he ever recognized my husband as the Radio Pastor. But if he came across a recent magazine article he may have recognized me.

KENWORTHY: And why should that have driven him to kill your husband?

FRAU PAGENDARM: I told you, he was a very great friend of the other man.

KENWORTHY: You mean the one you knew as Tradern?

FRAU PAGENDARM: Yes, but his real name was—

KENWORTHY: I know this is horrid for you, Frau Pagendarm—

FRAU PAGENDARM: His real name was the same as mine.

KENWORTHY: You mean that it was not true that your husband bought himself a new identity from the organization through which you escaped?

FRAU PAGENDARM: He was offered one, but he was not satisfied with it. My husband was an exacting man with a hawk's eye for detail.

The camera shifted now to take in Kenworthy full face.

KENWORTHY: You mean that he needed Tradern's — Pagendarm's — pay-book and other papers?

Back to close-up of Frau Pagendarm. Again she did not answer—but there is an informative way of not answering. And many viewers may have thought throughout this interview that she had no mean talent as an actress.

Crucible was on the tape, the tape was on the reel, the reel was on the master-console. And Posnan was setting his stop-watch for the first complete run-through when the message came to him on Home Counties TV's nearest approach to an internal hotline that a judge in chambers had granted an interim injunction against the showing of the programme.

'Bugger your bloody luck, chum,' Kenworthy said.

Four days later, Mitchell phoned. It was all tied up—he believed. They had never thought that there was much chance of tracing Lerche through immigration or movement records. There were too many hundreds of thousands involved. They hadn't a current name for him, no description that was likely to be of much use. There was no reason to know whether he would have gone back to Germany; or where.

They found him, as it were, from the opposite direction: a drunk and incapable picked up in Hamburg-St Pauli who had not been able to give coherent account of himself, even twenty-four hours after the alcohol had been pumped out of him. But it was not a case of amnesia. It was the guts that had gone from him, the life-purpose. He was between sixty and seventy and had no more fight in him, cared for nothing. Warmth, food, persuasion, a modest tot or two of spirits, had tapped the basic human need to confess.

Lerche had been wounded in the affray in the pine-fringes, the night that Tradern was killed. He had been nursed by the daughter of the farmer on whose land they had been cached: and who had herself lost a husband and two brothers. Hopelessly out of touch with Fromm now, protected by the freemasonry of a remote peasant corner, he had cut his losses, stayed with the woman, settled down to subsistence labour in a community depleted of its men. It was over thirty years later, when the woman died, that he found an illicit way out to the West, mostly out of wandering idleness, because his second world had tumbled about him. It was only when he recognized Anna-Maria in the magazine that he connected the Radio Pastor with the other Pagendarm that he had known. Then the demon of disgust seized him and his life found a new temporary purpose. He located Schultze, studied the pattern of the man's life with burning commitment: followed him to London on one of his occasional visits, thinking it might be safer to strike in a land as remote from his experience as that.

'So that ties it up,' Mitchell said.

'Does it? Not in my book. I once told Anna-Maria that we got a shade nearer the facts every time we met. It's perhaps as well that we shan't be meeting again.'

'What new riddles are you on about now, Simon?'

'Helmut Schultze was a bureaucrat killer—never an executive. I don't believe he had it in him to fire those shots himself. Whatever Lerche might have supposed, I don't think that trigger in the pine-woods was pulled by a man.'

'There's a lot of supposition there, Simon. But I'll drop a hint the way of the Germans, for what it's worth. If there's any more truth to be got out of Anna-Maria, it's up to them.'

'And the best of German luck to them!' Kenworthy said.